A House Divided

Bernard Marin

First published by Busybird Publishing 2025

Copyright © 2025 Bernard Marin

ISBN:
Paperback: 978-1-923216-94-5
Ebook: 978-1-923216-95-2

This book is copyright. Apart from any fair dealing for the purposes of study, research, criticism, review, or as otherwise permitted under the Copyright Act, no part may be reproduced by any process without written permission.

Enquiries should be made through the publisher.

This is a work of fiction. Any similarities to actual places and characters are a coincidence.

Cover image: Busybird Publishing
Cover design: Busybird Publishing
Layout and typesetting: Zoë Voss @ Busybird Publishing

Busybird Publishing
2/118 Para Road
Montmorency, Victoria
Australia 3094
www.busybird.com.au

More praise for
A House Divided

Bernard Marin's eminently readable novella tells a very contemporary story. A story that matters.

Set against the daily headlines and the social media tsunami which have engulfed our awareness of the Israel–Gaza war, we meet an Australian-Jewish family we can recognise. In streets and suburbs we know. And in language all too familiar. Where the generations clash, passionately and sometimes bitterly, about fundamental beliefs and values. But where they keep on talking, arguing, and confronting each other. Not just about Israel, Zionism, and the Palestinians, but about an inverted world.

Marin's comprehensive research makes the case for Israel and the Jewish people speak for itself, just as his empathetic ear for dialogue brings us a new guide for perplexed families. It offers them help to navigate their way, old and young, from generation to generation, through the thickets of our anxious and dangerous times.

Sam Lipski AO
former Editor-in-Chief
Australian Jewish News

In *A House Divided*, Bernard Marin invites readers into the intimate yet deeply charged conversations of a close-knit Jewish family grappling with the complexities of Israel, identity, and political conscience.

The novella captures the tensions that arise when generational experiences and external influences shape diverging perspectives on Israel's place in Jewish life.

As the family navigates these difficult discussions, the son's insistence on attending pro-Palestinian rallies – rife with extreme rhetoric – reveals the ease with which political activism can drift into anti-Semitism.

A House Divided explores the line between legitimate debate over Israel's policies and criticism distorted by ideological bias and anti-Semitic tropes.

Through the lens of this family's discourse, the novella serves as both a mirror and a corrective – challenging the prejudice of the zeitgeist and encouraging a deeper engagement with historical and contemporary realities.

Mark Leibler AC

National Chairman of the Australia–Israel and Jewish Affairs Council and Governor of the Australia–Israel Chamber of Commerce. He also serves on the Board of Governors and Executive of the Jewish Agency for Israel and the Board of Governors of Tel Aviv University. In 2025, he was awarded the Presidential Medal of Honour, Israel's highest civilian award, by Israeli President Isaac Herzog.

For my wife, Wendy,
daughters, Amy and Rachel,
daughter-in-law, Deb,
son-in-law, Joel,
and grandchildren, Goldie, Ziggy,
Millie and Andie.

Contents

1. Community service   1

2. Gays for Palestine   19

3. The error of your ways   25

4. A right-wing nutter   67

5. A missing definite article   87

6. A Zionist spy   113

7. Somewhere neutral   145

Acknowledgements   149

About the author   151

By the same author   153

I

Community service

'In the matter of the Crown versus Joshua Levine, Mister Levine please approach the bar table.'

Rachel rose and accompanied her nephew Josh to the table. Aged in his early twenties, he was clad in a rumpled blue denim shirt and jeans. His dreadlocks needed a trim, and he gazed up at the magistrate with green eyes through tortoiseshell glasses too large for his narrow face. He looked the part of a student radical from Central Casting, and that's exactly what he was in reality.

'Mister Levine,' intoned the magistrate, 'you are charged on summons with one count of obstructing police, one count of violating the *Graffiti Prevention Act 2007,* one count of damage to property and one count of public nuisance. How do you plead?'

'Rachel Levine for the defendant, Your Honour. Mister Levine pleads guilty to violating the Graffiti Prevention Act and damage to property. To the charge of obstructing police and public nuisance, he pleads not guilty.'

'And have the Crown and the defendant met to try and hammer out a mutually agreeable resolution to this matter?' asked the magistrate.

'We have, Your Honour,' chorused Rachel and the police prosecutor almost in unison.

The magistrate nodded his wigged head. 'Very well, we'll proceed to a contest mention hearing. How does … September 17th sound?'

'That's fine by the Crown, Your Honour,' replied the police prosecutor.

'Your Honour, the 17th falls within Rosh Hashana, the Jewish New Year. Would it be possible to reschedule?'

The magistrate examined his computer screen for a long moment. 'Would the 23rd be satisfactory?'

'Yes, thank you, Your Honour,' replied Rachel.

The magistrate glanced at the police prosecutor, who nodded assent.

'Very well, we'll reconvene on September 23rd at 11am. In the meantime, the Court would very much appreciate it if the defendant and Crown would meet again to try and resolve this matter beforehand. Case adjourned.'

'So … any chance of your nephew listening to reason?' asked the prosecutor as they walked out of the courtroom into the corridor.

'Any chance of dropping the obstruction and public nuisance charges?' countered Rachel.

'You know the charges to which he pleaded guilty can carry a six-month term of imprisonment?'

'Oh, please,' snorted Rachel. 'I've been a barrister for twenty years, so don't try and bullshit a bullshitter. No way a magistrate will hand down a custodial sentence for a first offence. Try again.'

The prosecutor sighed. 'Okay, we'll agree to drop the obstruction and public nuisance charges if you accept a two-year good behaviour bond and one hundred hours of community service on the graffiti and damage.'

'Deal,' replied Rachel. She extended a hand and they shook.

'Great. I'll draw up the paperwork and email it to your chambers.'

Rachel nodded. 'Thanks. I'll get it back to you quick smart.'

She looked over at her nephew, who was wrapped in an embrace with a wispy, short-haired girl in her early twenties.

'C'mon, Josh, let's go.'

Josh disengaged and glanced at his aunt. 'Where?'

'My chambers. We're meeting your mother there.'

'Okay, but Miryam is coming too.'

'No way,' growled Rachel. 'We have things to discuss that are … sensitive.'

'Things that concern her as well,' replied Josh as he smiled into his girlfriend's eyes. 'We have no secrets between us.'

'Fine.' Rachel rolled her eyes in frustration. 'Let's move.'

They walked along William Street to a Victorian stucco building with Doric pillars flanking a large oak door. But the heritage exterior of the building was belied by the ultra-modern interior of the foyer. Waiting for them was Josh's mother Sarah. The two sisters exchanged a look, then the four of them took a lift to level four and walked through a doorway bearing a brass sign that read *Plunket Chambers.*

Snaking their way past two rows of workstations, they strode into an office marked *Rachel Levine Barrister at Law*.

'Sit,' Rachel instructed, gesturing to a group of chairs placed in front of a large oak desk piled high with manila folders. She threw herself into the large executive chair and leaned back with a long sigh.

'We got them to drop the obstruction and public nuisance charges but Josh has had to accept a two-year good behaviour bond and one hundred hours of community service on the graffiti and damage.' She gave a wry smile.

'Could be worse,' said Sarah. 'Thanks, Rach.' Then turning to her son she snapped, 'What the fuck, Josh?'

'We—' was all Miryam got out before falling silent before Sarah's incandescent glare.

'This is between me and my son,' Sarah snapped. 'You're only here on sufferance, so I'd advise discretion as the better part of valour. Understood?'

Miryam nodded and Sarah turned her glare on her son.

'So again, Josh … what the holy fuck?!'

'What do you mean?' he responded, his tone truculent.

'What do I mean?' Sarah barked before pointing to a framed photograph on the wall. 'That's what I mean. Your father's cousin. He liberated the Kotel … the Western Wall … during the Jordanian occupation in 1967. And you're doing the functional equivalent of spitting in his face and the faces of all his friends who died during the liberation of Jerusalem. And then there are your grandparents and your community as a whole …'

'What about Bubbie and Zaydie?' Josh challenged.

'How do you think they'd feel if they knew their grandson was speaking at a pro-Hamas protest rally? That you were arrested after vandalising an MP's office? A Jewish MP, at that!'

'I like to think they'd be opposed to the genocide in Gaza,' Josh riposted.

'And then there's me,' Sarah sat back. 'I went with you to your doctor's appointments when you were transitioning, I sat at the foot of your bed when you had your mastectomy, and I cared for you when you came home from hospital. We went together to the Byron Bay Writers Festival, remember? And many other venues where you were invited to speak about your book. That I was proud as punch is an understatement. When you were nominated for Young Victorian of the Year for your work with *Minus 18* in support of young LGBTQIA+ kids, I stood tall next to you.'

'True,' muttered Josh. 'But how is any of that—'

'And now I feel betrayed.'

'The protest wasn't pro-Hamas; it was pro-humanitarian!' replied Josh. 'We were demonstrating in support of Palestinian human rights!'

'Yeah?' challenged Rachel. 'You and your "comrades" were chanting, "From the river to the sea, Palestine will be free", right?'

Josh nodded.

'In the original Arabic, that chant goes "From water to water, Palestine will be Arab."

It means the same thing Hamas says in its Covenant, that Israel is to be destroyed and its Jews slaughtered. Your grandparents would be horrified, as are we.' She nodded at her sister.

'I don't agree with—' Josh began.

'And don't get me started on that agreement between Sydney University and the Muslim Students Association!' Rachel interjected.

Josh sighed. 'What about it?'

'It's appeasement, nothing more, nothing less. It means the Muslim Students Association and their Jew-hating pals from Stand4PalestineAus can nominate a representative to a working group to review the university's investment policies in exchange for vacating their encampment on campus.'

'So what? It restored peace to campus.'

'Stand4PalestineAus has ties with the Islamist group Hizb ut-Tahrir. They're a terrorist organisation that's been banned in the UK and Germany. They applauded the October 7 slaughter of Israelis and urged Muslim nations to eliminate Israel.'

Josh glanced at Miryam, then turned to his mother. 'How can you possibly know they are linked to Hizb ut-Tahrir?' he demanded.

Sarah stared at her son through tired blue eyes and sighed. A twenty-two-year-old philosophy major at Monash University, what did he know of life?

Miryam added, 'You must understand the broader anti-colonialist context of October 7. Seven hundred thousand Palestinians were expelled from their homes in 1948 to make way for the State of Israel …'

'Did they cover how the 1948 War of Independence started in those woke teach-ins on campus?' snapped Sarah. 'Did they tell you that the Palestinian Arabs rejected a UN partition compromise and launched what they openly described as a war of annihilation against the Jews? Did they mention that the leader of the Palestinian Arabs, the Grand Mufti of Jerusalem Amin al-Husseini, spent the Second World War in Berlin hobnobbing with the likes of Hitler and Himmler? Did they mention that he was granted an audience with Hitler?'

'What has the Grand Mufti got to do with anything?' Joss demanded.

'He was the most senior religious and political leader of Palestinian Muslims,' replied Sarah. 'Did you know any of those things?

'Well … no, we didn't,' said Josh, 'but I don't see how it's even relevant. Just because you can link him to Hitler, so what?'

'Well, did your professors talk about the 900,000 Jewish refugees who, over the decade following Israel's War of Independence, were expelled from across the Middle East? Those Jews were forced to leave their homes in Morocco, Tunisia, Iraq, Syria, Algeria and Yemen and escape with the shirts on their backs to Israel, where they were absorbed into society.'

'It still doesn't justify driving Palestinians from their land in 1948.'

'And what about Israel's conquest of the Golan Heights, the West Bank and Gaza in 1967?' Miryam added.

'*Uti possidetis juris*,' replied Rachel.

'Huh?' They looked blank.

'A rule of customary international law that goes back to ancient Rome. In modern times it's been applied to the decolonisation of the Spanish empire in South America. To avoid interminable wars among newly independent nations over territory after imperial collapse, it was decided that each new country should have the provincial borders that existed under the colonial system. Do you know what that means in the context of Israel?'

Josh threw his hands into the air.

'That's why you should have taken my advice and studied law rather than philosophy,' Sarah interjected.

'Give it a rest, Mum,' Josh sighed. 'I told you a million times that I didn't want to become a lawyer. Our family has enough doctors and lawyers. We're such a Jewish stereotype. And anyway, it's not too late for you, if you love the law so much.'

'I'm quite happy with my publishing career, thank you,' said Sarah as she leaned back in her chair.

'But back to my point about international law,' said Rachel, 'what were the borders of the British Mandate?'

Josh shrugged.

'The answer is all Israel proper, plus the West Bank and Gaza. Which, in turn, means that the Jordanian annexation of the West Bank in 1949 was invalid. So, the Israeli victory in 1967 simply restored the borders in force during imperial rule under the British Mandate. *Uti possidetis juris* means that Israel has a legal right to all territory west of the Jordan River.'

'But hang on, only about a third of the population of the British Mandate were Jewish, weren't they? So by your logic, Palestinians should be entitled to claim land under your uti-whatever-it-is. And at no stage was the territory west of the River Jordan marked out for exclusive Jewish use. What about the UN Partition Plan? And why am I only hearing about this now?' Josh challenged. 'Why aren't the Israelis making this argument?'

Rachel sighed. 'They made a strategic mistake after the Six-Day War. In part because of international pressure and in part because the Israeli Left was opposed to keeping the West Bank. As a result of that error, Israeli governments have spent the last fifty-five years arguing that the wording of UN Resolution 242 doesn't require a total withdrawal from all territories captured in 1967. It was a boneheaded move, although that's easy to say with hindsight.'

'But what about the United Nations?' Josh protested.

'What about it?' countered Sarah.

'Well, the UN has deemed Gaza to be occupied territory even after Israel's withdrawal in 2005.'

'Total and complete nonsense,' Rachel snorted. 'Take out your phone and Google the 1907 *Hague Regulations Respecting the Laws and Customs of War on Land.*'

Josh tapped away at his phone before looking up. 'Okay, got it.'

'Now go to Article 42 and read aloud,' Rachel prompted.

Josh cleared his throat before reciting, 'Territory is considered occupied when it is placed under the authority of the hostile army. The occupation extends only to the territory where such authority has been established and can be exercised.'

'The Hague Regulations are the foundational treaty that governs the conduct of war,' explained Sarah, 'not the politicised nonsense churned out by the non-democratic regimes that dominate the UN. As you just said, Israel withdrew from Gaza in 2005, which means that on the morning of 7 October 2023, Gaza wasn't occupied.' Rachel exchanged a look with her sister.

'It may as well be,' Josh declared. 'Palestinians need permits from the Israeli military to do almost anything, visit family, a doctor—'

'Oh, spare me!' snapped Sarah. 'On October 7, one thousand Israeli civilians were butchered, shot at point-blank range, many after being gang raped. Whole families were burned alive. Babies were killed and over two hundred people kidnapped … and not only by Hamas's armed wing. At least four other armed groups from Gaza streamed through gaps in the fence to loot, murder and rape women and girls in Israeli communities. And the terrorists filmed their atrocities and posted footage on the internet. Crowds of Palestinian civilians cheered when hostages were led through the streets of Gaza. Think of all that before you get teary-eyed over Israel's response to the greatest one-day slaughter of Jews since the Holocaust.'

Josh glanced at his phone. 'Mum, we have to go, we're running late. Can we continue this later at home?'

'Fine,' sighed Sarah. 'But continue it we will.'

'Thanks, Aunt Rachel, for all the, you know,' Josh said, going around the desk to drop a kiss on her head.

'Goodbye, Mrs Levine,' murmured Miryam, her eyes downcast.

'Goodbye, Miryam,' replied Sarah in a chilly tone.

2

Gays for Palestine

'How're you going?' Josh asked Miryam as he unlocked the door of their South Yarra flat.

'Your mum hates me,' Miryam sighed as they trooped up the stairs to their bedroom.

'Well don't worry about that,' smiled Josh as he enveloped her in a bear hug. 'I love you enough for both of us.'

'Your mum is …'

'Relentless?' Josh suggested.

'And your aunt is scary.'

Josh laughed.

'I don't know whether it's because I'm Lebanese, or because I'm a lesbian in a relationship with a trans man ...'

'Does it matter?' smiled Josh.

Miryam shrugged. 'I suppose not. But her views on the Palestinians are ... tribal.'

'She's been very involved in Jewish community issues for years.'

'And the Palestinians be damned,' Miryam muttered.

'My mum was the leader of Melbourne Betar during high school.'

'What's that?' she asked.

'It's a right-wing Zionist youth group founded by Jabotinsky,' replied Josh.

'Jabotinsky?'

'A Zionist who had a lot to do with establishing the State of Israel.'

'Figures,' Miryam snorted before casting an apologetic smile in Josh's direction. 'Sorry, she's still your mum.'

'She is and I love her ... despite our differences. Besides, you and your parents haven't agreed on everything. Remember how they weren't exactly over the moon when you came out.'

'Arabs don't tend to be very tolerant when it comes to being gay.' She sighed.

'Or trans,' added Josh.

'Or trans,' echoed Miryam. 'And that's why I've never introduced you to my family. They'd freak.'

'Do you think they'd hurt you?' asked Josh as a worried frown spread across his face.

'You mean, like in an honour killing?' Miryam asked.

Josh nodded.

'Not my family,' she replied with a shake of her head. 'My mum and dad are Maronite Christians. They were educated in France. They're much too openminded for anything like that.'

'That's one thing I dislike about Arab culture,' said Josh, 'the homophobia.'

'It's a problem,' sighed Miryam. 'But we need to be careful about generalisations. And being suckered in by Zionists who use Israel's progressive gay rights policies as a propaganda weapon. They contrast Israel to the condition of gays in Arab society to score political points.'

'Well even you have to admit that there's something ridiculous about Gays for Palestine,' Josh chortled.

Miryam chuckled. 'We can't let the perfect be the enemy of the good. The homophobia and misogyny of Arab society is a secondary issue that we'll deal with later. After we've dealt with the primary problem.'

'Which is Israel?' prompted Josh.

'You mean the Zionist entity,' Miryam chided. 'Don't dignify it by using that name.'

'Whatever.' Josh shrugged.

'What do you mean "whatever?"' Miryam challenged. 'The biggest issue is settler-colonialism in all its forms. That's what we need to destroy in Australia and throughout the world.'

'So why don't we start here at home?' challenged Josh. 'Why start with Israel?'

'Because Israel is low-hanging fruit by comparison with the other settle-colonialist countries like the US, Canada and …'

'Australia,' Josh interjected.

Miryam nodded. 'Most definitely Australia, because First Nations sovereignty has never been ceded. But we start with Israel because it's much more doable.'

'You reckon?' Josh said dryly, then held up his palms in a gesture of surrender. 'But I'm a bit conflicted. I have family in Israel. Where are they supposed to go?'

'Back to where they came from!' snorted Miryam. 'Or they can live in the new state of Palestine alongside the Arabs in peace.'

'That would be nice,' murmured Josh, 'But not as nice as this.' He reached to embrace his girlfriend and a silence descended over the flat as they kissed.

3
The error of your ways

'Where's the fire?!' Josh yelled as he pulled the front door closed behind him. 'What's the big emergency?'

He was standing in the foyer of a large yellow-brick house overlooking Brighton Beach across the Esplanade. Built during the late 1930s in Bauhaus style, the home was a multi-million-dollar property in one of Melbourne's most coveted suburbs. Just the sort of place where one would expect a power couple orthopaedic surgeon and publisher to live.

'In your mother's study.' A loud bass voice echoed through the house.

Josh made his way through the hall to a room lined with floor-to-ceiling bookshelves. His mother Sarah and father Michael sat behind a large wooden desk with expectant expressions on their faces.

'What's this, an intervention?' Josh challenged.

'Just a conversation,' replied Michael Levine, his mouth curled in a conciliatory smile.

'A likely story, Dad,' Josh snorted. 'Mum has already given me the cross-examination treatment. Do we really have to do this again?'

Josh's father and mother exchanged a long silent glance before Michael turned to face his son.

'You're breaking your mother's heart,' Michael said with a sigh.

'A broken heart doesn't count for much when compared to the broken bodies of Palestinians in Gaza,' Josh growled. 'October 7 was bad, but the Israeli response has been totally disproportionate. Over forty thousand Palestinians killed by Israeli bombs and shells!'

Michael shook his head. 'Those are Hamas numbers. Do you really think an organisation that orchestrated mass rape and slaughter would hesitate to falsify casualty figures? Even if that number's correct, and I have my doubts, according to Israeli sources that number includes around twenty thousand Hamas terrorists killed in combat. I'm not going to shed any tears for those savages.'

'Those are Netanyahu's figures, I think you'll find,' Josh said, his eyebrows lowered in a stubborn frown. 'Do you really think that someone capable of bombing schools and hospitals and slaughtering civilians would hesitate to falsify casualty figures?'

'So tell me this,' pressed Sarah, ignoring him, 'why did those anti-Israel demonstrations begin immediately after October 7? That was three weeks before the Israeli ground incursion into Gaza.'

'Because the IDF began to conduct air strikes within hours of the October 7 attack.'

'So the Israelis suffer a massive terrorist attack and have no right to respond?' Sarah snorted. 'They should suffer in silence?! That's just anti-Semitism, pure and simple.'

'Rubbish,' snapped Josh, 'it's too easy to roll out that old complaint every time anyone criticises Israel. It's possible to distinguish between being Jewish and Zionism,' he went on patiently, 'and criticise the latter without attacking the former.'

'It may be possible, but the lines seem to get awfully blurred for many,' Michael said. 'What's your girlfriend think?'

'Miryam says Israel is a colonialist project and the process of decolonisation can only be achieved through armed resistance,' Josh said.

'Another woke slogan,' sighed Michael. 'I've read Frantz Fanon as well. So, do you want to know why your colonialist mantra is rubbish?'

Josh shrugged, as his mother took control of the conversation.

'Number one, there was no sponsoring foreign power,' Sarah interjected. 'Australia was established as a prison colony by the British government of George III and the Virginia Company was chartered by King James I. But Zionist immigrants arrived in the land of Israel against the wishes of the imperial rulers of the day – the Ottomans and then the British.

'Number two, the Zionist movement wasn't created to exploit the natural resources of a colony for the benefit of a mother country. Instead, it was devoted to finding a haven for Jews facing persecution.

'And number three, the Zionists didn't arrive in the land of Israel to serve as local elites who would dominate a native population. They came as penniless refugees driven out of their homes in Europe and the Arab world. The entire ethos of the early Zionist movement was based on hard physical labour by Jewish pioneers.'

'That still doesn't make Zionism just,' Josh insisted. 'It's an apartheid state just like South Africa.'

'Absolute tosh!' spat Sarah. 'Apartheid is segregation by race. It's when a minority rules over a majority through legal segregation and discriminatory laws for the benefit of that minority. At the end of 2024, Israel had about 9.3 million people. That population was made up of about 75 per cent Jews, 20 per cent Arabs, and 5 per cent others: all having equal civic rights. By comparison, in 1990, South Africa had a White government, with 75 per cent of its populace Black with barely any rights. Do you understand the difference?'

'You're talking about Israel. What about Gaza? What rights do the Palestinians who live in Gaza have?'

'The Israelis withdrew from Gaza in 2005,' Sarah retorted. 'Too often, Israel, with its 20 per cent Arab minority, is accused of apartheid, while those same accusers never mention the fact that in many parts of the

Arab world it's impossible to live as a Jew without being bullied, expelled or murdered by a mob. Palestinian President Mahmoud Abbas has declared that any future Palestinian state must be completely free of Jews and he imposes harsh penalties on any Arab who sells land to Jews. That's real apartheid.'

'But—' Josh protested, before Sarah silenced him with a wave of her hand.

'Let me say something,' Michael interjected. 'Arab Israelis who stayed in the newly formed Jewish state are full Israeli citizens. They have the right to vote, even electing Members of the Knesset who are openly anti-Zionist. They're doctors and nurses in Israeli hospitals. Hell, I conducted operations with Arab surgeons at Hadassah Hospital when we spent our Sabbatical year in Jerusalem.'

'The chairman of Israel's biggest bank is named Samer Haj-Yehia, an Israeli Arab,' added Sarah. 'There was no way in apartheid South Africa that a Black or Coloured doctor or pharmacist would have been allowed to treat Whites or be chairman of a bank.'

'Maybe, but it doesn't mean there's no racism in Israel.'

'Of course not,' sighed Michael. 'Israelis are humans with all the usual human failings. Show me any society anywhere at any time without individuals who have bigoted opinions.'

Sarah nodded. 'In 2017, a debate was held at the United Nations Human Rights Council. Diplomats from various Arab countries accused Israel of apartheid, ethnic cleansing, terrorism and discrimination. The final presentation was made by Hillel Neuer, the Canadian lawyer who stood up and pointed out that previously the Middle East was full of Jews; Algeria had 140,000 Jews, Egypt had 75,000 Jews, Syria had tens of thousands of Jews and Iraq had over 135,000 Jews. He concluded by asking, "Where's the real apartheid?" It's great viewing. You should watch it.'

Josh hesitated. 'Maybe.'

'And what about the United States and Australia?' challenged Michael.

'What about them?'

'Both America and Australia were founded on colonialism and ethnic cleansing,' replied Michael. 'After outright slavery was abolished in the US in the 1860s, racial segregation in the South persisted for almost a century by means of Jim Crow laws. And those policies were endorsed by the US Supreme Court. Here at home, First Nations peoples were only included in the census after the Referendum of 1967. But nobody questions America's or Australia's right to exist.'

'Some of my friends do,' grinned Josh.

'Silly far-Left fringe dwellers,' Sarah said, unamused. 'But no one in mainstream politics does so. Yet the demand for Israel's dissolution has become commonplace on the Left. Why?'

'I don't agree with you, but supposing you're right, one reason could be because of the 2018 Nation-State Law that enshrined the country's Jewish character, just for starters,' Josh said.

'I've already explained how the apartheid slur is countered by day-to-day life in Israel,' sighed Michael.

'But you still can't deny that Arabs are treated differently from Jews,' Josh insisted. 'Even their language is no longer "official".'

'In areas that relate to national security, sometimes,' Michael conceded. 'But on the other hand, Arabs aren't conscripted into the Israeli Defence Force, which means they get a three-year head start in life as opposed to Jews who do military service. They can start uni at eighteen while Israeli Jews have to enrol two or three years later.'

'I guess that's a valid point,' Josh conceded.

'The whole apartheid slur was invented by Amnesty International,' added Sarah. 'You should read *Israelophobia* by Jake Wallis Simons. He describes their campaign to appropriate the word apartheid and link it to

Israel through mass mailouts, street stunts, official reports and a social media blitz.'

'Well, I heard Amnesty joined Human Rights Watch and B'Tselem in accusing Israel of apartheid. What a bunch of rogues,' Josh said wryly.

'You may be right,' said Sarah dryly, 'it's all politics. Look at Tibet. It's been subjected to a long and brutal Chinese occupation since 1951. The Tibetan language and culture are outlawed and any attempt at expressing Tibetan national identity is crushed. Even wishing the Dalai Lama a happy birthday or having a Tibetan flag on your phone will make you a criminal. The country has been flooded with Chinese immigrants, outnumbering Tibetans in their own state. Worse still, nearly a million Tibetan children have been separated from their families by the Chinese and indoctrinated in boarding schools.'

'I thought you always told me two wrongs don't make a right,' Josh replied. 'The world is full of injustice. What is your point?'

'My point is, there's no widespread campaign to boycott Chinese goods and musicians,' said Sarah. 'Chinese students at Australian universities aren't bullied and accused by their lecturers of being agents of a racist foreign regime that's engaged in ethnic cleansing. But Israeli goods are boycotted and Jewish students are subjected to criticism. My point is there's a double standard where Israel is concerned.'

Josh looked at his mother and said, 'None of this changes the fact that the 1948 war was an exercise in ethnic cleansing.'

'And who started the war?!' Michael snapped, his conciliatory tone replaced by palpable annoyance. 'We talked about this already!'

'Is that so?' Joshua retorted. 'I just saw a documentary about a massacre committed by Israeli soldiers in the village of Tantura during the 1948 war. The film included first-hand testimony by Israeli veterans, now in their nineties, who confessed to murdering prisoners, raping and looting. So much for the myth about the superior moral standards of the Israeli military!'

Sarah shook her head. 'The story of Tantura isn't cut and dried. It's entirely plausible that some Arab prisoners may have been executed after the battle by individual Israeli soldiers, but historian Benny Morris argues that there's no credible evidence of an orchestrated large-scale massacre.'

'And other historians like Adam Raz argue that oral testimony by former Tantura residents is legit,' Josh insisted. 'Sooner or later, Israel will have to reconcile with its dark past.'

'I challenge you to show me a war in which there were no crimes committed by individual soldiers or small units fighting on the righteous side,' said Michael. 'During the Second World War there were incidents where American and British troops shot Germans who were trying to surrender. Especially after the SS massacre of US prisoners during the

Battle of the Bulge. And then there's the debate over the Allied bombing campaign against German cities. Do those issues undermine the justice of the Allied cause? Does anyone seriously demand that the UK and United States should be dismantled? Aside from your goofy friends, that is.'

Josh rolled his eyes. 'First of all, not everyone is demanding that Israel be dismantled. And second, there's a difference between individual soldiers and a campaign to drive a people from their land.'

Sarah shook her head in frustration. 'Think of it this way … there's no denying that some Israeli commanders expelled the inhabitants of hostile Arab villages along major supply roads. But that was due to military necessity during an existential defensive war. Remember that Israel at the time was under attack by seven Arab armies. And it's the sort of thing that's common in warfare. I'm also willing to concede that in a few cases Israelis may even have committed atrocities. But those crimes were aberrations from the norm. They don't amount to orchestrated and planned ethnic cleansing as your anti-Semitic friends claim.'

'Anti-*Israel*,' Josh stressed. 'Not every criticism of Israel is anti-Semitic!'

'I bet they never mention the far more numerous atrocities by Arabs against Jews that took place during the war,' Michael growled. 'Like the Arab massacre of Jewish prisoners at Gush Etzion, and the slaughter of Jewish doctors and nurses in the Hadassah Hospital convoy – two examples among many.'

'I thought the Hadassah Hospital convoy was attacked in retaliation after the Deir Yassin massacre,' Josh said, 'but what's the point in comparing atrocities?'

'The fact remains that about 150,000 Arabs accepted Ben-Gurion's offer of equal citizenship,' Michael replied, 'as written in Israel's Declaration of Independence.'

'Some of his other comments weren't so welcoming.'

'For example?' Sarah demanded.

'Ben-Gurion vowed that displaced Palestinians would never come back to their homes, didn't he? He said, "The old will die and the young will forget."'

'But it would have been suicidal madness for Israel to allow the return of an Arab population that had already proved itself hostile,' replied Sarah.

'Have you read Simha Flapan? *The Birth of Israel*? He quotes Ben-Gurion as saying that once the State of Israel was established, they'd expand it to include the whole of Palestine.'

'And did he?' challenged Sarah.

'Sorry?'

'Did Ben-Gurion conduct an aggressive war to conquer the whole of Palestine?'

'Well … yes,' said Josh. 'That's the story of the 1967 War.'

'Except that Ben-Gurion retired from politics in 1963. Four years before the Six-Day War. But hey, don't let the facts get in the way of your anti-Zionist narrative!'

Josh rolled his eyes. 'Come on, as if he didn't still have enormous influence and authority!'

'I'm familiar with Flapan,' said Sarah. 'He's a far-Left radical politician, so whatever he wrote has to be seen through that ideological prism.'

'Just as anything your favourite writers might say has to be seen through their ideological prism,' snapped Josh. 'Look, you can spin it any way you like, but Israel has an oppressive military that wields unnecessary force in response to minor attacks.'

'I love you, kiddo,' sighed Sarah, 'but it's absurd for a philosophy student who's never even picked up a weapon to be passing judgment on what is, or is not, unnecessary force in wartime.'

'And what about you?' snapped Josh. 'Are you now a weapons expert?'

'I'm a publisher who has read a great deal more history than you have,' said Sarah. 'And it's obscene to describe October 7 as minor.

It was the largest slaughter of Jews since the Holocaust. So you tell me, Mister Expert, what would be a proportionate response to such a pogrom?'

'Not killing forty times as many people,' Josh said, looking her in the eye.

An uncomfortable silence settled over the room that was broken moments later by Michael.

'Anyway, tell me what's so special about the Palestinians?'

'I don't understand what you mean,' Josh replied.

'You're upset about the Nakba?' Sarah interjected. 'The dislocation of Palestinian Arabs during the Israeli War of Independence?'

'Expulsion, more like it,' said Josh.

Sarah shrugged. 'Okay, have it your way … expulsion. Do you know what was happening in Eastern Europe at the same time?'

Josh seemed on the cusp of saying something but remained silent.

'Ever heard of Königsberg?' asked Michael. 'Over half a million ethnic Germans were exiled from their homes where their families had lived for centuries.'

'Presumably as part of the changes following the Second World War and Nazi aggression?' Josh said, raising an eyebrow.

'Königsberg was the capital of East Prussia,' Michael continued. 'Know what it's called now?'

Josh didn't respond.

'In 1946, the Russians annexed East Prussia and changed the city's name to Kaliningrad.'

'And your point is?' Josh replied, reaching for his phone.

'My point is that nobody is criticising the Russians for expelling half a million ethnic Germans—'

'Just as I thought,' said Josh, 'it was part of the Potsdam agreement, after the Second World War, which the Germans started. The Palestinians had done nothing …'

'And what about the Sudeten region of Czechoslovakia? It had a majority German population until 1945,' added Sarah. 'After the end of the war, three million ethnic Germans were expelled at gunpoint from the Sudetenland, with another twenty thousand killed during the process. So answer your father's question. What makes the Palestinians so special?'

'Well, they didn't start a world war, or slaughter millions of Jews for starters,' Josh snapped.

Sarah snorted in cynical amusement. 'So, how many Palestinians lost their homes in 1948?'

'Around 700,000,' Josh replied as an expression of apprehension settled over his face. Was he being set up?

'Correct,' nodded Sarah, reaching for her phone and doing a quick calculation. 'Compared to more than fifteen times the number of Germans expelled in Eastern

Europe. But no one is calling for a right of return of Germans to East Prussia and the Czech Republic. Why?'

Josh shook his head. 'I don't think your argument holds up to scrutiny. Your examples are all drawn from post-war resettlements between combatants. The Israel–Palestine situation is completely different. What had the Palestinians done that was equivalent to the Prussians or Germans?'

'I disagree,' Sarah replied. 'The mass expulsion of ethnic Germans post-1945 was at the behest of the Czech Government in Exile, who were preparing to establish an independent democratic Czechoslovakia. By contrast, the dislocation of Palestinian Arabs took place during a war in which Israel was fighting for survival against an attempt to annihilate the Jews.'

'They were Nazis!' Josh cried.

'All of them?' challenged Michael. 'Infants and small children as well?'

Josh snorted contemptuously. 'So do you think the kids should have been left there by themselves? Don't be ridiculous.'

'And anyway, it wasn't only ethnic Germans,' Sarah added. 'The redrawing of national borders after the Second World War caused the mass deportation of Ukrainians from Poland's newly acquired territories. Over half a million people. I already mentioned the 900,000 Jews expelled from the countries of the Middle East where their families had lived for centuries.'

'I still have no sympathy for those Germans. They were all Heil Hitlering until Germany began to lose the war.'

'You want to talk about Nazis?' challenged Sarah. 'Remember Amin al-Husseini? I mentioned him before.'

'Yeah.'

'He spent the war years in Germany recruiting for a Bosnian Muslim SS division and planning to export the Holocaust to the Jews of Israel if Rommel had won in North

Africa. So again, what's so special about the Palestinians?'

'That's one person! And how does that follow?' cried Josh.

'Heinrich Himmler promised al-Husseini that after Rommel defeated the British in the Middle East, the SS would extend the final solution to the Jews of Egypt, the British Mandate, Syria and Iraq.'

'Really?'

'Really,' Sarah nodded. 'In 1942, al-Husseini gave a speech at the opening ceremony of the Islamic Institute in Berlin where he insisted that the Jews had been enemies of Islam since Quranic times. He declared that they controlled both the United States and the Soviet Union. You sure this is the side you want to be on?'

'It's not about sides, and you're still talking about one individual, as if he represents all present-day Palestinians,' Josh protested. 'It's not that simple.'

'But it is about choosing sides,' said Sarah, 'which is precisely what your great-grandfather Samuel did in 1941.'

'Jeez, Mum,' moaned Josh. 'I've heard this story a million times!'

'And you'll hear it again because it's fucking relevant!' snarled Sarah with a ferocity that surprised her son. 'Your great-grandad was a twenty-nine-year-old doctoral student in law at Jagiellonian University in Krakow when the Germans invaded Poland. He went home to the town of Chelm and was rounded up with two thousand other Jewish males for a 30-kilometre forced march to a labour camp at the town of Hrubieszow. But your great-grandad wasn't one to be pushed arou—'

'I know,' Josh sighed, 'he escaped along the way and joined a partisan force in a nearby forest.'

Sarah nodded. 'Correct. And your great-grandfather fought with the Strzelecki partisans for three and a half years until the Red Army captured the area in 1944. And that's where he met Eva, who became your grandmother.'

'And after the war ended, they decided to leave Poland,' Josh recited in a robotic voice.

'They were the sole survivors of their immediate families and at first they tried to retrieve their family homes from the squatters now living in them. But they met with violent opposition from the squatters and indifference from the Soviet authorities. Yet it was only after the Kielce Pogrom of July 1946 that your great-grandparents decided to leave Poland.'

'Yes, I remember Grandma telling me that anti-Semitism ran deep in the heart of every Polish gentile and she would never return to Poland again.'

Sarah shrugged. 'In any event they sold what little they had and bribed their way past Czech and Austrian border guards into Italy. And there they connected with the Mossad Aliya Bet, the illegal migration organisation of the Jewish Yishuv in British Palestine. But their ship was intercepted by the Royal Navy and they were interned on Cyprus—'

'Which is where Bubby was born,' added Josh in a long-suffering tone.

'Correct,' said Sarah. 'After the British left in 1948, they finally made it to Israel and Samuel joined the army. He fought at the Battle of Latrun and was wounded. After the War of Independence …' she glared at her son in an unspoken challenge.

Josh refused to speak, then after a minute he said, 'You were talking about taking sides.'

Sarah ignored him. 'Your great-grandfather went about studying to qualify for the Israeli bar … which meant learning an entirely new language and system of jurisprudence, English common law. Samuel was just about ready to take the exam when notice arrived that his uncle Hershel – who emigrated from Poland to Australia in the mid-1930s – found out he survived the war. Hershel was a successful businessman in Melbourne and had the means to sponsor his nephew and family as immigrants.'

'But if Zionism is such a great thing, why did they leave Israel for Australia?' asked Josh.

'Not an easy question to answer,' replied his mother, 'but I suppose it was family that clinched the deal, so to speak. Both your great-grandfather and great-grandmother were the sole survivors of their families. Everyone else died from starvation in the ghettos, from a bullet at one of the massacre sites, or from gas at Auschwitz, Sobibor or Treblinka. They came to Australia to be with the only family they had left.'

There was a long silence, then Michael said, 'We've got sidetracked. The answer to the question of what makes the Palestinians so special should be "nothing".' He lifted his hands in a gesture of frustration.

'Can't you see what's happening all around you? Can't you see the injustice of demanding national self-determination for the Palestinians while simultaneously denying it to the Jews?' Sarah cried.

Josh shook his head. 'Nobody is demanding the destruction of Israel or denying the right to Jewish self-determination; they're demanding rights for Palestinians.'

'You sure about that?' she barked. 'Some of your girlfriend's social media posts say otherwise.'

'Have you been cyberstalking Miryam?' Josh demanded. 'Doing a bit of lurking?'

Sarah shrugged. 'Don't post on social media if you don't want people to see what you've written. But she's wrong on the facts. Hamas is open in its demand for the destruction of Israel—'

'But Hamas doesn't represent every Palestinian,' Josh insisted.

Sarah pressed on. 'Hamas aren't the only ones. Here in Australia, anti-Semitic incidents are up by over 700 per cent. Adass Israel Synagogue was firebombed and Jewish buildings in Sydney were defaced by graffiti.

Our community is living in fear. Why should a conflict in the Middle East generate threats of violence against Australian Jews?'

'Probably because the Australian Jewish community is enthusiastically Zionist,' said Josh.

'And the Australian Muslim community is enthusiastically pro-Palestinian,' Sarah retorted, 'but I don't see Jews threatening violence against Muslims and organising protest marches in front of mosques.'

'What about the Burgertory fire?' Josh asked. 'It triggered a riot in South Caulfield Park.'

'Another piece of anti-Semitic mythology,' interjected Michael. 'Turns out that the arson attack was the result of a commercial dispute. The two people charged with that crime are not Jewish and have nothing to do with the Jewish community. Yet, I've seen TV footage of pro-Palestinian rioters trashing parliamentary offices. You don't see members of the Jewish community acting in such a violent manner.'

'I guess that's true,' Josh conceded.

'And your bigoted comrades then go on to say the Jews are settlers who've stolen Palestinian land.'

'They're not bigots,' Josh protested, 'and it's indisputable that the Jews have stolen Palestinian land.'

'I beg to differ,' snapped Sarah, her face flushing with annoyance.

'They're protesting the theft of land in the West Bank!' Josh insisted.

'Utter crap,' Sarah muttered as she tapped away at her phone. 'But first I'm gonna read you the text of a letter sent by Simon Maccabee ... you remember the Maccabees from our Hannukah celebrations?'

Josh nodded.

'So, this is a message sent by Simon Maccabee to King Antiochus during the Jewish revolt against the Greeks. It was recorded in the *First Book of the Maccabees* during the second century BCE ...'

Josh rolled his eyes but said nothing.

'This is what Simon wrote: "It is not foreign land we have taken, nor have we seized the property of others, but only our ancestral heritage which for a time had been unjustly held by our enemies." In other words, here we have a Jewish leader living over 2,000 years ago asserting a claim to the land of Israel in a letter to a foreign king. So again, can you name me any Palestinian leader who lived even 150 years ago?'

'What does that prove?' Josh repeated. 'The Hebrews were always fighting somebody, so presumably, there were other tribes who believed they had a right to the land.'

Sarah continued. 'It proves the Jews are indigenous to the land of Israel. We've had an unbroken presence there for 3,500 years. The Kingdoms of David and Solomon. The Hasmonean Kingdom. The Bar Kokhba Revolt. Even after most of us were expelled by the Romans, there was still a strong Jewish presence in the land. By contrast, the Arabs only showed up in the seventh century when they conquered the land of Israel at sword point from the Byzantines. So, who are the natives and who are the foreign imperialists?'

'That's rubbish. Herodotus wrote about Palestine even before your Simon Maccabee. And what about the Canaanites?'

Sarah ignored him. 'By your argument the Aborigines have the right to this land and we should all find somewhere else to live. So should most Americans, and lots of others. That's what your girlfriend believes. Are you seriously proposing that as an argument? Have you packed your bags for a return to Poland? That's where we come from originally, you know.'

'I'm not talking about Australia right now,' growled Josh. 'I'm talking about the Zionist entity.'

'You mean Israel,' spat Sarah.

'You call it what you want and I'll call it what I want. And the fact is that Jews and Palestinians both spring from Canaanites and are closely related genetically. I don't think you can argue for the history of the Jewish connection to the land and deny the connection of the Palestinians. The Old Testament describes many battles between the Hebrews and others. Who were those others?'

'Vanished from history,' fired back Michael. 'Those *others* to whom you refer are the long-disappeared people cited in the Torah – the Canaanites, the Amelkites, the Midianites, and many others. Those civilisations haven't existed for thousands of years. Those names have no more connection to modern Palestinians than the ancient Assyrians do to modern Syrians.'

'That's right, let's ignore DNA when it suits …'

'Don't believe the hype,' Sarah interjected. 'The Arabs were a foreign culture from the Arabian Peninsula that has no link to the vanished city states of the Torah.'

'Make up your mind, Mum,' barked Josh. 'You're now arguing from two contradictory positions. On the one hand, you say invaders everywhere have the right to conquered land …'

'Not true,' Sarah interjected.

'Let me finish my point!' snapped Josh. 'And on the other hand, you argue that the Jews have been in Israel forever and have a right to the land. But you don't extend that principle to the Palestinians. Mum, you can't argue the long history of the Jewish connection to the land and deny the connection of the Palestinians.'

'I can and do deny it. Before the British Mandate the Land of Israel was just another imperial province under the Ottoman, Mamluk and Byzantine Empires.'

'But Mum, that proves nothing. It was populated by Palestinians. You don't discount the Jewish population just because they were under Roman rule. The genetic profile of Palestinians has been studied by scientists. They've proved that Palestinians and other Middle Eastern populations, like

Turks, Lebanese, Egyptians, Armenians and Iranians, are genetically very close to Jews. Archaeological and genetic data support the belief that both Jews and Palestinians came from the ancient Canaanites, who extensively mixed with Egyptian, Mesopotamian and Anatolian peoples in ancient times.'

'So, now you're going to argue that Palestinian–Jewish rivalry is based on cultural and religious, but not genetic differences?' pressed Michael.

'If you like, but I'm pointing out that Jews and Palestinians are closely related and no doubt occupied the same territory over millennia. Jews and Palestinians both spring from Canaanites and are closely related genetically. The relatively close relationship of Jews and Palestinians to Western Mediterranean populations reflects the continuous mixing of culture and genes that has gone on for millennia. In other words, it's not just Jews who have occupied Israel for millennia.'

'I know more than a bit about genetics,' said Michael, 'and even if that's true, it has nothing to do with the longstanding relationship between the Jewish people and the land of Israel.'

'Then you'll have to explain why the Jews are more entitled to the land than others who also have an equally long attachment to the land,' Josh declared.

'But where are those others of whom you speak? Where are the Persians, the Assyrians, the Byzantines, the Mamluks and ... yes, the Crusaders? The only ethnic people who retained their national identity over the centuries and millennia are the Jews.'

'National identity?' challenged Josh. 'There was no Jewish nation until 1948. We were scattered to the four corners of the earth – we were Ashkenazi in Europe, Sephardic in Spain, Mizrahi in the Middle East and Africa ... we were Black in Ethiopia, Brown in India, and White in Europe. And I'm not talking about the Byzantines or the Assyrians.

The Arab population was twice the size of the Jewish population in 1948.'

'No denying that,' Michael nodded, 'but you omit the fact that they were mostly immigrants from Egypt, Syria and other neighbouring Arab countries who moved in during the early twentieth century.'

'So you say. Where's your proof?' Josh said, annoyed. 'That can't be true. If most of the Arabs arrived in the early twentieth century, who were the Arabs living there under Ottoman rule?'

'Actually, I can,' replied Sarah, 'on the basis of British population records and even the most common Palestinian names. For example, the surname "al-Masri" is quite common in Gaza. Know what it means?'

Josh shook his head.

'It means "the Egyptian",' explained Sarah. 'So, someone named Muhammad al-Masri is Muhammad the Egyptian. A clear indication of where that family comes from.'

'Or came from once. And those population records?' Josh started typing on his phone as his mother spoke.

Sarah nodded. 'The census figures collected by the British Mandatory authorities show high child mortality rates among the local Arabs. So high that, I suspect, the tripling of the Arab population within Mandatory Palestine could not have occurred because of natural birth rates.'

'So you're, what, a demographer, a medical expert? And where do you get the tripling of the Arab population? It says here that under the Ottomans, Muslims made up 85.5 per cent of the population in 1878! Then under the mandate, the vast bulk of immigrants were Jewish. Look, according to these figures, the Muslim population *decreased* from 78 per cent in 1922 to 61 per cent in 1944. You just make things up!' He shoved his phone back in his pocket, shaking his head.

'My point still stands. Why is the descendant of an Egyptian family who moved to Mandatory Palestine for economic reasons more worthy than the descendant of a Jewish refugee escaping anti-Semitic persecution?'

'We've already dealt with that.' Josh hauled out his phone and woke the screen. 'It's rubbish. Only 11 per cent of the population were Jewish in 1922 and 78 per cent were Muslim. By 1931 that figure had dropped to 73 per cent and the percentage of Jews had risen to 17 per cent, so who were the migrants?'

Sarah looked at Michael and shrugged, for once lost for words.

'You slip and slide from one point to the next, but you are seriously begging the question. The tripling of the Arabs couldn't be because of natural birth rates? Spare me.'

'So, what am I, chopped liver?' challenged Michael with a broad smile. 'I may be just an orthopaedic surgeon, but I've learned a thing or two being married to your mother for over thirty years.'

Josh rolled his eyes. 'Like what? And what are you even trying to say? That the Palestinians have no rights? Your arguments make my head spin.'

'Depends on what you mean,' replied Sarah. 'It's not my personal view, but after a hundred years of terrorist violence, some people argue the Palestinians have forfeited any moral claim to independence.'

'That's outrageous!' Josh said. 'And haven't you just been telling me how good the Israeli Arabs have it? How free and independent they are?'

'Why is it outrageous?' asked Michael.

'Because not all Palestinians support terrorism. And terrorism just might be the only weapon available to a small population facing the IDF, backed by the might of America. Nobody calls the Viet Cong terrorists these days since they beat the US.'

Sarah shook her head. 'Again, I beg to differ. You make the common mistake of looking at this through the prism of Western values.

You fail to understand that Hamas is the Palestinian arm of the Muslim Brotherhood, which means that for them this is jihad. They see it as a religious war that takes priority over everything else, including the wellbeing of the Gazan people. That's why billions of dollars in international aid that was supposed to fund homes, schools and clinics was spent on weapons and tunnels. And that's not even considering the hundreds of millions lining the pockets of Hamas leaders in Qatar and Turkey. Did you know that Ismail Haniyeh's net worth was said to be four to five billion dollars, Khaled Mashal is worth three to five billion and Mousa Abu-Marzook's net worth is said to be three billion? Yasser Arafat was said to be worth two hundred million when he died.'

'That proves my point. The Palestinians remain dirt poor while Hamas grows rich. Anyway, I'm suspicious of those figures,' Josh said.

Sarah's mouth curled in a cynical smile. 'Oh really? It's been documented beyond doubt that Arafat's widow, Suha, lives in Europe on a multi-million-dollar fortune she inherited from Yasser. And she's been charged with corruption by the Tunisian government.'

'Look, I don't know anything about this woman or her fortune, and anyway, it's irrelevant,' Josh said, annoyed. 'My point stands. Not all Palestinians support Hamas or terrorism. But can we continue this another time? This interrogation has gone on long enough, don't you think?'

'Fine,' replied Michael. 'But we're not done here. Your mum and I promised the family that we'd try to make you see the error of your ways.'

'Right back atcha,' Josh snorted. 'I think you're the ones in the wrong here. But I'm gonna go home now. We can carry on the debate at a later time … if you insist.'

'Oh yeah, we insist,' Sarah nodded. 'You'd better believe it.'

4

A right-wing nutter

'You're done for the day,' announced the crew supervisor.

Josh sighed and unsnapped the hi-vis vest he was obliged to wear while performing his community service assignment – graffiti removal. As he returned his equipment to the van, the supervisor sent a smirk in his direction.

'A bit of cosmic justice, eh? Maybe next time you'll think twice about defacing public property.'

'Yes, sir,' Josh replied in a monotone. Picking a fight would be stupid. 'May I go now?'

'See you next week,' the supervisor sneered.

Josh turned on his heel and walked toward the 58 tram that would take him to Flinders Street Station and the train home to Brighton. It was Friday afternoon, and he found himself yearning for a home-cooked meal.

He arrived at Platform 4 less than a minute before the 6:14 to Sandringham was scheduled to depart. The trip to Brighton Beach took just over a half hour and he reached his family's front door just before 7:00. Well before the time to light the candles that marked the beginning of Shabbat dinner.

'In here,' his mother shouted from the kitchen as the front door slammed shut.

Josh passed through the dining room and noticed the table was set for a dozen diners.

'We have guests?'

'Yeah,' replied Sarah without turning away from the kitchen bench on which she was busily chopping up tomatoes and cucumber for the salad. 'Your Aunt Rebecca and co.'

'Oh, jeez!' Josh moaned. 'Malka spent a semester at Tel Aviv University and thinks she's the world's greatest expert on the Middle East. And she's a right-wing nutter. This is gonna be worse than that struggle session you and Dad put me through last week.'

'If being a Betarnik makes Malka a right-wing nutter, what does that make me?' his mother said as she cast a cheeky grin over her shoulder.

'At least you present relatively rational arguments,' sighed Josh, 'most of the time. Malka just parrots the line that God gave the Land of Israel to the Jews, full stop. That's her whole case.'

'It's a position with which I have some sympathy,' said Sarah. 'Besides, she's your father's niece and your cousin. But now I want you to go jump in the shower before they arrive. You stink.'

'Yes, Mum,' Josh muttered. He made his way up to his old room, whose walls were still painted in their original feminine pink, a vestige of life before transition.

Freshly showered, he made his way downstairs toward the sound of lively chatter emanating from the dining room.

'Hello, Josh.' Rebecca Greenbaum, an elegant woman who looked in her early fifties, smiled at him. The resemblance to Michael was obvious.

'Hi, Aunty,' Josh replied, leaning forward to deliver a kiss to Rebecca's offered cheek.

'Malka.' Josh nodded to a dark-haired young woman in her early twenties.

'How are you?' Malka replied in a tone that indicated indifference to any answer that might be forthcoming.

'Not bad,' said Josh. 'I'm putting the finishing touches to my master's thesis so I have to decide whether to leave it at that or go on to do a PhD.'

'If you can stay outta gaol, you mean,' Malka snorted. 'How much time do you owe on your debt to society, anyway?'

'Three more hours and I'm done,' said Josh tersely, 'as if you give a shit.'

'Stop that right now, both of you!' Rebecca chided. 'Malka, you promised to be on your best behaviour. Don't disappoint me.'

'Sorry, Ima,' said Malka through gritted teeth. 'It's just …' her voice trailed away, leaving her sentence unfinished.

Josh's father appeared wearing a bright blue kippa and motioned for all assembled to take their places around the table. Bottles of kosher red were opened and Michael led the gathering in the blessing over the wine followed by the blessing over the bread.

'Is this hallah from Glick's?' Malka asked as she tore off a piece of braided egg bread.

'Homemade,' smiled Sarah.

'Yummy,' said Malka between mouthfuls. 'You'll have to give me the recipe.'

'Of course, dear.'

'So … Josh … are you done with your community service?' asked Malka as her mouth curled in a not-so-innocent smile.

'Malka, stop,' urged Rebecca. 'Don't make a scene.'

Josh cast a defiant grin across the table at his cousin. 'Don't fret, Aunty. I've nothing to be ashamed about.'

Malka snorted her contempt.

'And as a matter of fact, I'm almost done, as Malka well knows, since I told her about five minutes ago.'

'The real question is whether you've learned your lesson,' snapped Malka. 'Somehow I doubt that.'

'And what lesson is that?' asked Josh with mock sweetness. 'One that sings the praises of Jewish racial superiority?'

'We talked about this,' sighed Sarah. 'The issue isn't skin colour, DNA or racial heritage. It's culture. Have you ever noticed the total absence of democracy among the twenty-one

Arab nations of the Middle East? They're all dictatorships or monarchies, or killing each other in a civil war like Syria or Yemen. No government for, of and by the people. No free press. No independent courts. Ever wondered why that is?'

'You're being racist,' muttered Josh. 'They have their own culture. Democracies are not ordained by God. Look at what's happening in the so-called greatest democracy on earth!' he added scornfully.

'That's just stupid,' snorted Malka.

'Your cousin is right,' intoned Sarah. 'It's wrong to call me a racist, but I'll happily cop to being a culturalist. It's obvious that Westminster democracy is superior to Wahhabi theocracy, and we shouldn't be afraid of saying it loud and proud.'

'That's right,' piped up Malka. 'Are you gonna argue that the inferior treatment of women in Arab culture is legitimate?'

'The gender debate is a distraction,' said Josh. 'The war in Gaza is the most pressing issue. Over forty thousand innocent Palestinian civilians have been killed!'

Sarah frowned. 'Well, as a female professional and a feminist, I view the dignity of women as non-negotiable.'

'Geez, Mum, I feel like I'm getting the third degree,' Josh complained. 'It's four against one and you're all jumping from one point to the next.'

'We're just fleshing out the facts versus your opinions,' Sarah smiled. 'While the death of any non-combatant is a tragedy, you have to ask yourself who is responsible.'

'The Israelis, of course!' Josh cried. 'They're the ones dropping the bombs!'

'Not true,' replied Sarah, 'the fault lies entirely with Hamas, Palestinian Islamic Jihad and the Gazan civilians who broke into Israel on October 7 to pillage, abduct and loot. Without October 7, this war wouldn't have happened. And it would end tomorrow if Hamas were to release all the Israeli hostages and surrender. But again, the leaders of Hamas are quite happy to sacrifice their own people at the altar of jihad against the Jews. There's also the issue of human shields.'

'Oh please,' groaned Josh, 'that's just an obscene excuse used by the Israelis to protect themselves from war-crime accusations.'

Malka shook her head. 'Your mum's right. The evidence is overwhelming that Hamas uses civilian homes, UN schools, mosques and hospitals for military purposes. And the same is true of Hezbollah in Lebanon. By firing rockets from those places and storing weapons there, they draw Israeli retaliatory fire. That makes those locations legitimate targets under the law of war. Also, they hide hostages in those places.'

'You can't get around the fact that forty thousand people are dead!' Josh cried.

'There's no reason to shout,' Sarah chided. 'As I said earlier, these are Hamas figures, and in any event, at least twenty thousand of them are terrorists. But there's no doubt the impact of the war on the innocent residents of Gaza has been terrible.'

'At least you admit that,' Josh snorted. 'But as to your figures of twenty thousand terrorists, what's your source for that if there are no reliable figures coming out of Gaza?'

Sarah sighed. 'There's never been a war where civilians haven't died. Take the Second World War, for example. You hate Nazis, right?'

Josh nodded.

'Around half a million German civilians died from Allied bombing as opposed to seventy thousand British civilians who died from German air attacks. The higher number of German civilian deaths doesn't mean the Nazis were the righteous party in the Second World War, does it?'

'Of course not!' Josh replied.

'Then why are you applying that argument to the Palestinians?' asked Sarah.

'I'm not,' Josh protested.

'But you are,' replied his mother. 'In fact, I'd say you've fallen for a cynical Hamas strategy of maximising Palestinian civilian casualties to maximise public support in the West.'

'Look, the UN recognises figures from Gaza's health ministry, and even the Lancet estimates the death toll as being higher than the official figures. The UN says most of the deaths are women, children and the elderly.'

'The UN,' snorted Malka.

There was a moment's silence as Josh raised his eyes to the ceiling as if asking for patience.

'Pull out your phone and look up the Palestinian Constitution,' Sarah said abruptly.

Josh shrugged, tapped away at his phone and announced, 'Okay, got it.'

'Look at Article Two,' Sarah instructed. 'What does it say?'

Josh focused on his phone screen for a moment before looking up. 'It says that Palestine is an Arab and Islamic nation.'

'Now look at Article One,' Sarah continued. 'Please read it.'

'It says, "Palestine is part of the larger Arab world, and the Palestinian people are part of the Arab nation",' Josh said.

'Now look at Article Four,' Sarah commanded.

Josh continued looking at his phone screen and said, '"Islam is the official religion in Palestine", and "The principles of Islamic Sharia shall be a principal source of legislation".'

'In other words, an ethnic and religious state, correct?'

Josh nodded.

'You'll find similar versions of the same thing in the constitutions of every other Arab country. So why are you and your friends advocating for an Arab Islamic Palestinian state, but against a Jewish state?'

Josh shrugged. 'That's not what I'm advocating. Like you, I support a two-state solution.'

'Dearest Josh, I'll always love you, but you've gone a bit astray here. As I told you before, prior to 1948 the land of Israel was a province of larger empires. The Ottomans ruled it for over four hundred years. Before that, the Mamelukes, the Crusaders, the various Arab caliphates and the Byzantines. When the British received their mandate from the League of Nations in 1922, it was a dual mandate on behalf of the Palestinians and the Jews. From the Jewish perspective, it was for the explicit purpose of building a Jewish national homeland.'

'But that triggered violence between the Jews and Palestinians,' Josh replied. 'So, was it worth it?'

Sarah's eyes widened. 'It was worth it to the Jews who managed to escape Europe before the gates were locked in 1939. Don't you understand that most Israelis just want to be left alone?'

Josh chewed on a cuticle. 'So, you're opposed to a two-state solution now?'

Sarah ignored him. 'In 1947, the Jews accepted the UN Partition Plan. But the Arabs rejected peace and went to war. You want to talk about genocide? Read the promises of massacre announced by Arab leaders after the UN vote.'

'A promise isn't genocide,' said Josh, 'and the partition plan was unfair. It gave most of the land to the Jewish minority.'

'Most of that Jewish allocation consisted of the uninhabited Negev Desert,' replied Sarah. 'But I would argue that's not the real reason for the Arab refusal. In 1937, the British Peel Commission proposed another partition plan that would have given the Arabs 85 per cent of Mandatory Palestine. They also rejected that proposal because 15 per cent for the Jews would have been 15 per cent too much.'

'But what about 1967? The Six-Day War began with a pre-emptive attack from Israel,' Josh said.

Sarah shook her head. 'Incorrect. The fighting began after Egyptian President

Nasser blockaded an international waterway to Israeli shipping. This was an act of war under international law. It cut off the Israeli port of Eilat to maritime commerce. Imagine if a foreign country blockaded the entrance to Port Philip Bay. Do you think Australia would just roll over and accept that?'

'Probably not,' Josh conceded.

'Well, that's what triggered the Israeli airstrike on the 5th of June 1967.'

'A war in which another 300,000 Palestinians were displaced and in which Israel conquered massive territory,' muttered Josh, 'the Golan Heights, the West Bank—'

'Wars have consequences,' interrupted Sarah.

'Sis, can we take a break from the geopolitical debating society and have our meal?' pleaded Rebecca.

'Of course,' nodded Sarah. 'Sorry.'

'I'll help,' volunteered Rebecca, and the two women disappeared into the kitchen, only to return moments later with trays brimming with beef brisket, roast chicken and a vegetable quiche for the non-carnivores in attendance.

The next twenty minutes passed in relative silence as the everyone focused on their meal.

At last Michael pushed his chair back from the table and emitted a sigh of sated satisfaction. 'That was delicious, Saraleh. I don't know how you do it.'

'Simple,' smiled Sarah. 'I brought home the manuscripts I had to read. So it was easy to take the day off and do a bit of cooking for tonight.'

'Sorry I couldn't help,' replied Michael, 'but I was in theatre from 7:30 to 1:00.'

'Given the level of your culinary skills, darling, that's not such a bad thing,' grinned Sarah.

Michael laughed, raising his hands in surrender. 'Darling, I'm aware of my limitations.'

'So Josh, what were you saying before about the West Bank?' Malka prodded.

Josh sighed. 'I was saying it was lost to Israel in the Six-Day War, and I'm asking why, if Israel wants peace so much, it has built settlements in the West Bank and East Jerusalem over the past fifty years. As we speak there are more than 700,000 Jews living in settlements that are illegal under international law.'

'Illegal according to whom?' asked Malka

'I just said – international law! Have you read the International Court of Justice ruling?' Josh reached for his phone. 'It says Israel has illegally annexed the occupied territories!' He struggled to control his anger, then went on more quietly, 'Most of the international community agrees that the Geneva Convention prevents an occupier from changing the current situation in an occupied territory.'

'Remember *uti possidetis juris*?' replied Sarah, ignoring his remarks about the ICJ.

'That's just convenient legal mumbo jumbo. You and Rachel apply it when it suits you, and ignore it the rest of the time. I've had enough of this! I came here for Shabbat dinner, not an Oxford Union debate! I'm going home!'

'Ah, Joshie, don't storm out,' his mother pleaded.

But Josh pulled his coat off the rack and slipped out the front door without another word.

He made it to the station mere seconds before the train to the city pulled away from the platform. The trip to South Yarra station took just over ten minutes and eight minutes after that he slipped his key into the front door.

'Is that you, babe?' Miryam's voice came from the bedroom.

Josh grunted in reply as he threw his coat over the back of the sofa.

Miryam appeared, clad in a Bugs Bunny onesie. 'Bad?'

'A goddamned inquisition,' growled Josh. 'I knew it was gonna be bad. But my fuckin' cousin was there and she's an absolute Ziofascist. She spent the last year studying at some yeshiva in Jerusalem. The way she talks makes Bibi Netanyahu look like a moderate.'

'So what happened?'

'Boom,' replied Josh, throwing his hand out. 'In the end, I had to do a runner.'

'Sorry, babe,' said Miryam as she nuzzled Josh's cheek. 'Families can be tough. But tomorrow night your mum will be interviewing that professor at Melbourne Uni. Do you wanna go?'

'Sure,' snorted Josh, 'if only so you can see the sorta cross-examination I endure anytime I go home.'

Miryam smiled. 'I got a taste when we were in your aunt's chambers after court. But it'll be interesting to see how she fares against Professor Keogh.'

'Who's he?'

'She,' Miryam corrected. 'She's a visiting professor from Trinity in Dublin who teaches international law. She's a big critic of the war in Gaza.'

'I wouldn't be betting against Mum,' said Josh as he shook his head. 'She's pretty determined, although the publishing house that she works for distributes the book in Australia, so she'll have to be a bit more circumspect or her boss won't be too pleased.'

'Professor Keogh is an internationally recognised scholar who consults for the UN. I think it's likely she'll make mincemeat of your mum … polemically speaking.'

'I hope so,' sighed Josh. 'At least I should be able to pick up a few debating points that might help me deal with my family.'

5

A missing definite article

Josh and Miryam stepped off the 58 tram at Haymarket Station and hurried along Pelham Street to the Melbourne Law School building. They pushed through the double doors to find the David P. Derham Theatre packed to overflowing. Not only were the auditorium's 300-plus seats filled to capacity, but the aisles were overflowing with students and members of the public. A photograph of Professor Keogh's latest book dwarfed the two women on stage, the title clearly visible – *Palestine: International Legal Perspectives*.

The discussion had begun and Josh recognised his mother's voice as he concentrated on threading his way through the people sitting on the steps. Spying a vacant spot two-thirds of the way down the aisle, he took Miryam's hand and moved to occupy it. Once seated, he focused on the stage and saw his mother seated on one side of a coffee table opposite a younger woman in her forties whose mass of unkept hair resembled a shrub that was overdue for a trim.

'But would you not agree that the Fourth Geneva Convention doesn't apply to Judea–Samaria?' Josh's mother asked in a calm, quiet voice that reverberated through the loudspeakers on either side of the stage.'

'You mean the West Bank?'

'You may call it that if you wish, Professor Keogh, but allow me to claim the same privilege. As I was saying, the Convention doesn't apply to Judea–Samaria because the

1949 to 1967 Jordanian occupation was illegal. It was never accepted as legitimate by the international community. Therefore, per *uti possidetis juris*, the Israeli capture of the West Bank restored the territorial integrity of the British Mandate.'

'The territory controlled by the British Mandate was never intended solely for Jewish occupation,' said Professor Keogh, her Irish lilt unmistakable. 'And the Convention explicitly applies to all armed conflicts. It makes no difference that the Jordanian occupation was unrecognised.'

'It makes all the difference in the world,' Sarah replied. 'The Convention applies to *enemy* territories occupied in wartime. The Jordanian occupation was illegal and therefore, per *uti possidetis juris,* was never legally severed from Israel—'

'A dubious legal theory that has never been tested in jurisprudence,' scoffed Professor Keogh. 'With respect, I think I know a little more about international law than my publishers.' A ripple of laughter passed through the audience. Josh could see a flush of annoyance creep up his mother's throat to her cheeks.

'If I might continue? The West Bank was not foreign enemy territory and thus, the Fourth Geneva Convention doesn't apply.'

'That I do not accept, but let us set it aside for now. General Assembly Resolution 242 explicitly recognises the West Bank as occupied territory captured in 1967.'

'Ah, but even 242 doesn't require an Israeli withdrawal from all territories. The text does not include the definite article "the" that would extend it to the entirety of the territories captured by Israel. And as US Ambassador to the UN Arthur Goldberg stated, that omission was deliberate. Hence the resolution is ambiguous as to precisely what territories are to be returned. And that's because of the obvious strategic considerations.'

'Are you serious?' challenged Professor Keogh. 'A missing definite article allows Israel to retain all the territories captured in 1967?'

Again there was a ripple of laughter, with one or two low boos and hisses.

'I mean the obvious indefensibility of Israel's pre-1967 borders. It was only fourteen kilometres from the Mediterranean Sea at Netanya to the Jordanian border at Tulkarem. In Melbournian terms that's about the distance from Box Hill to the CBD, or the distance from the Dublin GPO to Killiney. And the Jordanians held the high ground overlooking Tel Aviv and Israel's coastal plain. That's why it was the centre-Left Israeli Labor Party that established settlements along the Jordan Valley almost immediately after the guns fell silent in 1967. It was to give Israel the strategic depth that was lacking before the Six-Day War. The Labor Government of Levi Eshkol also re-established Jewish communities like Kfar Etzion, which were lost during the 1948–49 War of Independence.'

'And every one of them is illegal under UN Security Council Resolution 2334,' snapped Professor Keogh. 'The International Court of Justice rejected Israel's arguments on that matter as well.'

'The International Court of Justice is a highly politicised body that is an arm of the highly politicised UN,' snorted Sarah. 'And when it comes to Israel, both are polluted by bigotry and bias. Besides, the ICJ is only empowered to issue advisory opinions. It's a toothless tiger, which is a damned good thing given its anti-Israel bigotry.'

Josh turned to Miryam, shaking his head. His mum had clearly lost it.

'I find it appalling that you'd engage in such an attack on the international rules-based order,' said Professor Keogh. 'The United Nations is an essential institution in keeping global peace.'

'The UN is corrupt from top to bottom,' Sarah said furiously, 'and then there's UNRWA ...'

'What about UNRWA?' challenged Professor Keogh. 'It performs vital humanitarian work for Palestinian refugees!'

'Look at it this way,' said Sarah, her tone didactic, 'since 1950, all communities of people displaced by war or natural disaster have been assisted by the UN High Commissioner for Refugees, the UNHCR. UNHCR's mission is to provide immediate support and protection with the longer-term objective of third-country resettlement, and over the past seventy-five years, it has resettled over 50 million refugees worldwide. With one exception … the Palestinians. The Palestinians have their own agency that serves to prolong the conflict by perpetuating a sense of national victimhood …'

'So your answer is to turn all Palestinians into refugees and drive them from their homeland? And before you deny they have a homeland, under the British Mandate, 73 per cent of the population were Muslim; a mere

17 per cent were Jewish – that's in 1931. And are you going to deny that those Palestinians have been victimised by decades of Zionist aggression?!' demanded Professor Keogh.

'Indeed I am,' nodded Sarah. 'But I'm making a different point at present. From post-war Europe to the current conflict in Sudan, UNHCR has worked tirelessly to resolve refugee problems through resettlement and integration into new host societies. But UNRWA is a separate agency exclusive to the Palestinians that seeks to prolong the conflict with Israel by handing down refugee status from generation to generation. And I'm not even going to elaborate on the many, many UNRWA staff members who moonlighted as Hamas terrorists and participated in the atrocities of October 7.'

'Well, those are some pretty sweeping claims, Sarah, with no evidence to back them up.'

'You say there is no evidence, but that is not the case. As we all know, nine staff members were stood down because of their involvement in October 7.'

'Indeed, nine out of 32,000, and the UN said Israel had not provided enough evidence to support their claims of widespread corruption within UNRWA.'

Sarah gave a contemptuous snort. 'One staff member is too many, let alone nine.'

'Let me also say that UNRWA is not exclusively a refugee organisation – UNRWA stands for United Nations Relief and Works Agency – so the comparison with UNHCR is unsound. May I remind you, UNHCR stands for United Nations High Commissioner for Refugees. And while I'm sure there are many Israelis who would like to define all Palestinians as refugees and see them resettled in some neighbouring country, that's not how Palestinians see themselves.'

There was a small murmur of approval from the audience.

'Let's return to the more pressing issue of settlements,' Professor Keogh continued. 'You can make your … Likudnik arguments until the cows come home, but there's no denying the question of settlements is hotly disputed even inside Israel.'

'By a small and shrinking minority of Israeli Jews,' replied Sarah.

'Well, that's simply untrue,' replied Professor Keogh.

'The Israeli Left thinks the settlements are a disaster. But their political power has been on the decline for years. And it well-nigh vanished after October 7. Also, don't forget Israel withdrew unilaterally from Gaza in 2005, uprooting seventeen Jewish communities by force. Those Jewish residents didn't want to leave their homes.'

'But the Israelis retained control over Gaza's airspace, shared border and shoreline,' riposted Professor Keogh. 'That means Gaza was still occupied in reality.'

'I beg to differ,' said Sarah. 'After 2005, the Israelis never controlled Gaza's southern border with Egypt.'

'One border crossing!' Professor Keogh interjected. 'And that only open to Palestinians with permits approved by the Israelis!'

Sarah ploughed on. 'Hamas almost immediately started firing rockets into Israel. If October 7 proved anything, it's that Israel needs a stronger and more secure border.'

'A very one-sided view,' said the professor.

'The only side I care about is the side of factual accuracy,' replied Sarah.

'Oh really?' Professor Keogh snorted. 'You talk as if there's no intransigence and fanaticism on the Israeli side. Your right-wing extremists cost Israel perhaps its best chance of peace with the assassination of Yitzhak Rabin!'

'A tragedy,' agreed Sarah. 'But in retrospect, it's pretty clear that the Oslo Accords were a failure. Over a thousand Israelis were murdered by Palestinian suicide bombers during the Second Intifada. That was after a peace offer sponsored by Bill Clinton, which would have created a Palestinian state over almost all the West Bank. But Arafat rejected it.'

Professor Keogh leaned forward. 'That's because it was a one-sided proposal. But I'm less interested in what happened then as opposed to what's happening now. Those Israeli air strikes on heavily populated areas of Gaza amount to collective punishment.'

'Hamas uses its own people as human shields,' Sarah insisted. 'How else is the IDF to root out and destroy those responsible for October 7?'

Professor Keogh shook her head. 'Not like this. And it's against Israel's best interests. The IDF's actions have alienated the world.'

'You mean alienated the Left,' challenged Sarah. 'La France Insoumise, British Labour and the American Democrats are prime examples. Here at home, it's the socialist Left of the ALP and the Greens. And of course Ireland, where Jew-hatred runs deep.'

'Offensive and racist nonsense,' said Professor Keogh, her anger now obvious. 'The progressive wing of modern politics—'

'Progressive?' interjected Sarah. 'How is it progressive to support a bunch of jihadi fanatics whose moral value system leads them to support the medieval barbarism of October 7?'

'That's not a fair characterisation—' Professor Keogh stated more calmly.

Sarah shook her head. 'Professor, haven't you ever asked yourself why, when al-Qaeda attacked America on 9/11, the world was outraged, but when Hamas attacked Israel on October 7, very quickly the world turned against the victim?'

Professor Keogh leaned forward and said quietly, 'Because of Israel's disproportionate response to October 7 and the killing of innocent Palestinian civilians, of course.'

'And never mind that October 7 was the largest slaughter of Jews since the Holocaust?' challenged Sarah. 'Around 9,500 missiles, rockets and drones have been fired at Israel since October 7. And what about the hundreds of daily terrorist attacks over the years? In 2022 alone, Israel was hit with more than five thousand terror attacks ranging from stabbings to shootings and bombs ...'

Professor Keogh gave a wry chuckle. 'Oh please. Nearly three thousand were instances of people throwing stones. Do you really call kids throwing stones terrorists now? And that tally pales by comparison to the death toll in Gaza.'

'You might want to ask Yehuda Shoham about kids throwing stones,' replied Sarah, 'but you can't because he was killed in his car seat at the age of five months when a rock thrown by rioting Palestinian teenagers smashed the windshield of his family car.'

'I believe there have been similar tragedies in other countries, with kids throwing rocks from overpasses on freeways. Were they regarded as terrorist acts?'

Sarah abruptly changed the subject. 'Well, Professor, what in your view would be a proportionate response to October 7?'

'Not what Netanyahu has been doing. I believe that boycotting Israel is the only solution to this merciless bombing in Gaza and Lebanon, since they disregard international law and international sanctions.'

'Never gonna happen,' snorted Sarah. 'Most Americans support Israel in the current conflict ...'

'And your source is?' Professor Keogh demanded.

'Is a poll by Harvard University, which found that over 70 per cent of Americans thought that the IDF should complete the destruction of Hamas by attacking Rafah.'

'Not surprising in view of Donald Trump's re-election,' Professor Keogh replied. 'America is in the grip of neo-Fascism, and many of its people have never been very clear about world geography, let alone world politics.'

'You may hold that view,' sighed Sarah, 'but here are the facts about Israel's adherence to the law of armed conflict. Military lawyers vet each Israeli airstrike to ensure compliance with the laws of war. Mistakes are inevitable during the fog of combat, but the IDF goes above and beyond by warning Palestinians they should relocate. The problem is that Hamas doesn't allow them to leave because they're useful as human shields. There have been reports of Hamas firing on Gazans who are trying to follow Israeli instructions and leave the battle zone. As I said before, Hamas does not value human life.'

'Zionist propaganda, I think you'll find,' replied Professor Keogh.

Sarah shook her head. 'It's fact. Hamas has engaged in a strategy of human sacrifice that seeks to maximise Palestinian civilian deaths. The greater the death toll, the greater the international political pressure on Israel. At least that's what they believe. But the thing is, after October 7, the Israelis aren't interested in what international moralisers have to say. Their survival takes precedence over the carping of Irish anti-Semites.'

Professor Keogh let that remark hang in the silence, and Sarah shifted a little in her seat. An older bearded man climbed the stairs leading to the stage.

'Mum's boss,' said Josh. 'He doesn't look too happy.'

'Please give our participants a round of applause for a most spirited exchange,' said the man. After the applause he continued, 'And now we have around 15 minutes for questions from the audience. Please wait for the microphone to reach you before asking your question. And I use the noun question intentionally. No speeches, please. Begin by identifying yourself and keep it short and sharp with a question mark at the end. We'll start with the woman in the purple dress.'

A pause ensued while a young man handed a mobile microphone to a woman in her mid-twenties who was standing in the fourth row.

'Thank you,' she said. 'My name is Helen Moreland and I'm a graduate student in global politics. My question is to Ms Levine. Ms Levine, you seem to be arguing that the war in Gaza is existential for Israel. But given the disparity in military force in Israel's favour, is this argument really defensible?'

'Thank you for the question,' replied Sarah. 'I'm hardly an expert on Hamas, but I have read its charter. And in the wake of October 7, I think it's reasonable to take Hamas at its word. The Hamas Charter contains a laundry list of classic anti-Semitic tropes. It accuses the Jews of dominating the world through money; of causing the French and Bolshevik Revolutions and triggering both World Wars. It declares that Israel must be destroyed by armed force and cites an Islamic Hadith that calls for the murder of every Jew in the world.'

Helen Morland shook her head and lifted the microphone. 'I believe that was in the old charter that has been superseded. I think the new one accepts the two-state solution.'

'Incorrect,' answered Sarah. 'The 2017 Hamas Charter continues to call for the destruction of Israel. It maintains that the establishment of Israel was illegal and that they'll never recognise what they continue to call the Zionist project.'

Josh stood up and raised his hand.

'Thank you,' said the MC, 'and can we now go to … the young man in the left aisle?'

Josh waited until the microphone reached him.

'My name is Josh and I'm a graduate student studying philosophy. My question is to Ms Levine. How is anyone meant to get a full picture of what is happening when the Israelis are deliberately targeting journalists who might expose the IDF's crimes?'

'Thank you for the question,' said Sarah, maintaining a poker face. 'But I'm afraid it is based on a false premise. British journalist David Collier conducted a study into this issue and found that many of the journalists killed in Gaza were also terrorists. It turns out about

70 per cent of them published expressions of support on social media for the attacks against Israeli civilians. I remember the report mentioning a freelance photojournalist who urged Gazans on October 7 to grab a weapon and fight.'

'If I may,' said Professor Keogh. 'The IDF has stated publicly that it does not distinguish between some journalists and armed Hamas fighters. They refuse to provide evidence of those journalists they claim are Hamas soldiers. The US Committee to Protect Journalists say over one hundred Palestinian journalists and media workers have been killed in the war in Gaza.'

'It's been said the first casualty in war is truth,' replied Josh, retaining his grip on the microphone.

'Many of them were moonlighting as Hamas and Palestinian Islamic Jihad terrorists,' Sarah interjected. 'Collier's report featured the case of a journalist who was killed in the house of his father, a high-ranking

Islamic jihad commander. The house was targeted because of the terrorist father, not the journalist son. And then there was that Instagram post where two photojournalists from Gaza were boasting about having advanced knowledge of the October 7 attack. In that post, one of them is admiring footage on his friend's camera that shows the desecrated body of an Israeli soldier. There are even reports that one of these so-called "journalists" was an active participant in the kidnapping of Israelis. So bottom line there's no credible evidence that Israel has a policy of targeting journalists to hide war crimes that the IDF isn't committing.'

'Well, I don't see the logic of that remark,' Professor Keogh said mildly.

'What about the case of Shireen Abu Akleh?' challenged Josh.

'This will have to be the last exchange between the two of you,' said the bearded man. 'We have others waiting to ask their questions.'

'Thank you,' said Sarah to the moderator before looking squarely at her son. 'As it happens, I looked into the Abu Akleh case. The facts are that she was killed amid heavy fighting between IDF troops and Palestinian gunmen in Jenin, a city in Judea–Samaria that's known as a centre of terrorist activity. It's easy to judge from afar in Australia. The battlefield is a chaotic environment where mistakes are easy to make. In Gaza, there have been several incidents in which Israeli soldiers have killed their comrades by accident. So-called friendly fire. This happens in every war and there's no indication the shooting of Abu Akleh was anything other than a tragic combat error.'

Josh relinquished the microphone and sat down to a hug from Miryam, as Professor Keogh said, 'The IDF have acknowledged that Abu Akleh was shot in the head by one of its soldiers, but no disciplinary action was taken.'

'That was amazing,' said Miryam, kissing his mouth. 'I'm proud of you.'

'We're out of time so this will have to be the last question, said the moderator as he pointed to stage left. 'Let's go to the man in the fourth row with the brown sweater.'

'Thank you,' said the questioner who looked to be in his early forties. 'My name is Graham and I'm an assistant professor in the communications department. My question is to both of you and relates to the media as well. How would you justify Israel's decision to expel Al Jazeera from the country? How can this decision be reconciled with the democratic principles professed by Israel so often and so loudly?'

'Thank you for that question as well,' smiled Sarah, before Professor Keogh could reply. 'The simple fact of the matter is that Al Jazeera is a media network funded by the Emirate of Qatar, which is a major financier of Hamas. Demanding that Israel must allow what in essence is an enemy media outlet to function is the equivalent of demanding that Australia should have allowed the Reich Broadcasting Service to maintain a bureau in Canberra during the Second World War. It's absurd, as is the protest letter signed by hundreds of Australian journalists in defence of those jihadist propagandists.'

'But Netanyahu allowed the Qatari government to send millions into Gaza …'

'I'm afraid we'll have to conclude,' said the bearded moderator. 'Thank you all for coming, and thank you to Professor Keogh, visiting professor of international law from Trinity in Dublin, and Sarah Levine for a spirited discussion. Professor Keogh will be signing her latest book, *Palestine: International Legal Perspectives*, and there are copies for sale at the bookstall. Good night.'

Josh stood and watched his mother and Professor Keogh exchange a perfunctory handshake as Sarah's boss took her by the arm and led her off stage. The publicist approached

Professor Keogh, all smiles, and herded her towards the signing table. Josh turned to slip his arm through Miryam's and said, 'I think Mum's in for a roasting. I wonder if he'll sack her.' They shuffled along with the crowd out of the building onto Pelham Street.

'Where to?' Miryam asked.

'I'm hungry. You?'

'Don Tojo sounds pretty good,' she replied.

'Japanese it is,' Josh declared. 'Let's g—'

'Josh!'

He sighed and turned to see Sarah approaching along the sidewalk. 'Hi, Mum.'

'Hi, son. Hello Miryam,' she said with a nod. 'What are you guys up to?' She looked calm enough but her cheeks were still flushed.

'We were going to get something to eat,' Miryam said.

'Well, don't let me keep you,' said Sarah. 'I just wanted to ask Josh to come home tomorrow evening. Your father and I have something to tell you.'

'Another struggle session?' grumbled Josh.

'Please come home, Josh. It's important. I'll even cook your favourite.'

'Well, the prospect of chicken schnitzel does make the idea a bit more appealing,' Josh smiled.

'Thank you, darling,' said Sarah as she delivered a quick peck to her son's cheek.

As Sarah walked in the other direction, Josh exchanged a wry grin with his girlfriend. 'I think I'm gonna have some sake with dinner.'

The peals of their laughter echoed down the street as they strode eastward toward their destination on Cardigan Street.

6

A Zionist spy

'Home!' Josh's voice echoed through the hallway.

'In the study, son!' Michael yelled. 'Dinner's ready, but your mum popped out to get a few last-minute things before we sit down. She'll be back any minute.'

Josh's head appeared around the door jamb. 'Hi, Dad.'

'Come in and take a load off,' said Michael as he gestured toward the chair in front of his desk.

Josh sat as instructed.

'So what did you think of your mum's performance last night?'

'She lost her shit a bit. She's not usually abusive, especially with one of the firm's authors. I did want to ask her more about the media, but it wasn't the time or place last night.'

'What about them?' asked Michael.

'She says they're hopelessly biased.'

'And she's right. Case in point, Artsakh.'

'Arts-what?' asked Josh.

'A self-proclaimed breakaway state in Nagorno-Karabakh,' explained Michael. 'Three weeks before October 7 the Azerbaijani army attacked this enclave in the Caucasus that was populated by 150,000 Armenians, who fled. One hundred and fifty thousand people! And less than a month before the war in Gaza. You've never heard of it because no one cares. There was very little press coverage and no protests on the streets of the world's cities. As there were no Jews involved, nobody cared.'

Josh shook his head. 'You're being paranoid. Most people have never heard of Nagorno-Karabakh …'

'True,' said Michael. 'They think Georgia is a state in America rather than a country on the Black Sea. And who's heard of the Caucasus?'

'The lack of media coverage almost certainly comes from the fact it's a little-known place in a little-known part of the world. The fact there are no Jews there has nothing to do with it.'

'You just don't get it,' sighed Michael. 'Over the past decade, the civil war in Syria killed up to 600,000 people, of whom 307,000 were civilians. And now a former leader of al-Qaeda is running the country. Where is the mass public outcry over that?'

'Well, you can't say the atrocities in Syria weren't widely reported,' said Josh. 'And I don't think Jolani was a former leader of al-Quaeda, but let's not let facts stand in the way of some good propaganda.'

Michael abruptly changed tack. 'Your friends ignore Israel's rich history of cooperation with sub-Saharan Africa and the developing world,' he said. 'Soon after the State of Israel's creation, David Ben-Gurion believed the Black and Jewish communities had a bond in the fight against discrimination. However, that relationship started to erode in 1955 at the first Afro-Asian conference in Bandung, Indonesia, when a speaker at that conference was none other than Hitler's buddy, Palestinian leader Amin al-Husseini. Remember him?'

'Oh please, not al-Husseini again. Mum's been hammering me about him for days,' Josh said, pretending to pull out his hair.

'Okay, okay. Let's look at the UN then. The Arabs haven't been able to defeat Israel on the battlefield, so they've focused their hostility on the United Nations. Muslim nations have put financial and political pressure on developing countries to exclude Israel from key groups at the UN. It was only in the year 2000 that Israel was able to join the "Western Europe and Other" group at the UN. But by then the damage had been done. In 2019 alone, the General Assembly of the United Nations adopted eighteen resolutions against Israel, compared to seven against all other countries combined.'

'There's no denying that Israel bears the brunt of condemnation at the UN,' said Josh. 'But I'd argue it's for good reason.'

'And what reason is that?' Michael challenged.

'To condemn Israel's evil deeds, of course!'

'Are you really going to argue that Israel is the most terrible human rights abuser in the world today? In Saudi Arabia, there's a place called Chop Chop Square; it's been the site of public decapitations. In China, disappearances are normal, and Muslims are being captured and put into camps. In Iran, LGBTQI⁺ people are stoned to death.

In Syria, the regime of Bashar al-Assad used chemical weapons against its own people. Putin is a murderous thug. In Myanmar, the army is massacring the Rohingya Muslim population. I could go on all day. Former UN Secretary-General Ban Ki-moon conceded on the eve of his departure from office that there had been too many resolutions against Israel. Of course, he waited until he had one foot out the door before saying anything.'

Josh harumphed.

'It's more contemptible than funny,' Michael snapped. 'So, where are the demonstrations against Iran, Syria or Rus– ?'

The sound of the front door slamming interrupted the flow of Michael's words.

'Is Josh here?' Sarah's voice sounded from the entrance.

'In my office,' shouted Michael.

Sarah appeared. 'Come into the dining room. I'll have the meal ready in a moment.' She bent over Josh to deliver a kiss on his cheek. 'So what are you discussing?'

'Same old, same old,' sighed Josh, getting up and following her out to the dining room.

'This is a special occasion so I got a special something that will satisfy your sweet tooth,' Sarah said.

Josh smiled in anticipation. 'Chocolate?'

'Boutique chocolate,' replied Sarah. 'The best I've ever tasted.'

She pulled a dark brown box from her shopping bag and handed it to her son.

'Ika chocolate,' murmured Josh as he tugged the lid off the box.

'May I?' he asked, glancing up at his mother.

'One,' she smiled. 'Leave the rest until after dinner.'

Josh plucked an almond-topped chocolate from the box. After a moment of examination he popped it into his mouth.

'Mmmmmm,' he murmured. 'That has to be the best chocolate ever! Where'd you get it, Mum?'

'Feinman's Deli on Glen Huntly Road,' she replied.

'You mean the place that imports food and wine from Israel?'

'That's the one,' Sarah nodded, glancing over her shoulder as she went into the kitchen. 'And that "best chocolate ever" you've been praising was made in Tel Aviv,' she said as a parting shot.

'Of course it was,' said Josh rolling his eyes.

'Yep,' nodded Sarah, bringing out the first course, 'it's owned by a woman from my year at Scopus. She went to Israel for a year on the Taglit program, married an Israeli, and has lived there ever since. I attended their wedding at the Western Wall in Jerusalem back in the day.'

'So?' prompted Josh.

'You may not remember because you were young, but about ten years ago, the usual rabble of Melbourne Leftists and Islamists mounted protests at an Israeli-owned chocolate dessert bar called Max Brenner.'

Josh sighed. 'Mum, you know that if I'd been an adult back then I would have been part of that rabble.'

Sarah shrugged. 'Now it seems that your friends want to mount a boycott against Feinman's because it carries Israeli products. That's BDS in action – Boycott, Divestment and Sanctions. Targeting people because of their Israeli ethnic origin. It's disgusting. But sit down, eat. Eat.'

'Is the owner of this deli a Zionist?' Josh asked.

'Of course he is,' replied Sarah. 'Like so many in our community, he has family in Israel. His niece was raped and killed on October 7. So do you think he deserves to be boycotted?'

Josh looked down at his plate but said nothing.

'The BDS movement peddles lies and hypocrisy,' Michael interjected. 'They promote economic sanctions against Israel. But when you scratch the surface, BDS activists are just opposed to Israel's existence.'

'I don't think that's right,' Josh protested. 'It's a movement about justice.'

'Justice?' snorted Michael. 'The founder of BDS is a bloke named Omar Barghouti. He says that no self-respecting Palestinian will ever accept the existence of Israel. How just is that?'

'I don't blame him,' said Josh. 'After all, Israel has been attacking the Palestinians for over seventy years. Case in point, the past few months.'

'Always in self-defence,' insisted Sarah. 'BDS is just a modern version of the Arab Boycott.'

'The what?'

'After Israel was created, the Arab League established a Boycott Committee that put financial pressure on countries and international companies to avoid doing business with Israel. The boycott began to crumble after Egypt made peace with Israel in 1979.'

'But there's no moral obligation to do business with people you don't like!' Josh insisted.

'That's true,' Sarah conceded, 'but have a look at Israel's history. Look at 1967. Within six days Israel had won the war,' Sarah said.

'And stolen new territory,' Josh complained.

'Spoils of a defensive war,' Sarah replied.

'And all the while, the Israelis continued building illegal settlements on the West Bank,' Josh cried.

'I've already addressed the issue of legality many times,' sighed Sarah, 'but even in Judea–Samaria the Israelis have repeatedly shown a willingness to forfeit territory for the creation of a Palestinian state in return for peace.'

'Not true!'

'Sorry,' Michael interjected, 'but as US Senator Daniel Moynihan once said, you can have your own opinion but you can't have your own facts. The Israelis allowed Yasser

Arafat and thousands of Palestinian terrorists into Judea and Samaria …'

'Thousands of terrorists?! I don't believe this. And Dad! I insist you call it the West Bank,' said Josh.

'Potato, potāto,' shrugged Michael. 'Into the West Bank, then. And when President Clinton tried to seal a peace deal just before leaving office in January 2001, Arafat refused and launched the Second Intifada. Do you know what Clinton said to Arafat after the talks collapsed?'

Josh shrugged.

'Clinton said, "I'm a colossal failure and you made me one." The Second Intifada was a four-year bloodbath of suicide bombings that killed over one thousand Israelis. Even then, a few years later Prime Minister Olmert offered the Palestinians an independent state. But that Israeli peace proposal was rejected as well. The sad reality is that the Palestinians place greater importance on preventing Jewish independence than they do on gaining their own. They've been knocking back compromise peace proposals since 1937. I would argue they're the authors of their own misfortune.'

Josh gave a sigh and slid down in his chair, then, abruptly changing the subject, said, 'So, tell me this, how would you distinguish between criticism of Israel and anti-Semitism, since the former always seems to be regarded as the latter whenever we argue?'

'Good question.' Michael nodded. 'Natan Sharansky suggested three markers to distinguish between legitimate criticism of Israel and anti-Semitism – three Ds: demonisation, double standards and delegitimisation. First is the belief that Israel is a demonic force of unique evil. The second is judging Israel by a separate standard. Third is the belief that Israel has no right to exist as the nation-state of the Jewish people.'

'Wasn't this Sharansky a minister in a right-wing Israeli Government?' Josh asked.

'I'd call it a conservative government, but yes,' Michael conceded. 'Picking up on his double-standard point, United Nations records show that numerous wars, injustices, human rights abuses and atrocities taking place all over the world are disregarded and yet Israel is criticised. It's blatant hypocrisy.'

'No it isn't,' said Josh with a shake of his head. 'The fact that the International Criminal Court has arrest warrants for the leaders of Hamas and Israel is proof that everyone is subject to the same standards. There's no anti-Semitism.'

'Yeah,' snorted Sarah, 'never mind all those Hamas leaders are dead! But do you really think the elected leaders of a democracy should be treated the same way as leaders of a jihadi terrorist group that carried out the October 7 massacres? Don't you see how warped that is?'

'And yet it was okay to bring the elected leaders of the German democracy to court in Nuremberg?' Josh asked. 'Israeli leaders should be called to account for any war crimes they've committed,' he added. 'No one should be above the law.'

Sarah shook her head and sighed. 'I've already explained to you how the Israeli military goes above and beyond the requirements imposed by the laws of war. If an individual Israeli soldier commits a war crime, they're court-martialled. If a Hamas fighter commits a war crime, he gets a monetary bonus. Speaking of bonuses, are you familiar with the Palestinian Authority's "pay for slay" program?'

'What's that?' asked Josh.

'The PA pays lifetime salaries to terrorists who conduct attacks against Israelis. And the size of those payments increases with the number of Israeli casualties. In other words, kill more Jews, get more money. And if the terrorist dies in the attack, his family receives a pension for life.'

'So, you're saying the Palestinian Authority is subsidising terrorism?' challenged Josh.

'Those are pension payments to the families of Palestinian prisoners, that's all.'

'In other words, a financial inducement to terrorism,' Sarah snapped. 'The PA also educates children to hate Jews. The Palestinian equivalent of *Playschool* teaches toddlers and primary-school students to seek martyrdom against the Jews. It's disgusting!'

Josh's brow rose in a sceptical arch. 'Sounds like propaganda to me, but even if it's true, it's just an inevitable response to seventy-five years of Israeli aggression. You can't blame the Palestinians for resisting colonial oppression.'

Sarah emitted a sigh of despair. 'The late Chief Rabbi of Great Britain, Lord Jonathon Sacks, described anti-Semitism as a "shape-shifting virus". He said that in the Middle Ages, Jews were hated because of their religion. In the nineteenth and early twentieth centuries we were hated because of our race. We were hated because we didn't have a state ... the Soviets described us as "rootless cosmopolitans". And now we're hated because we do have a state. Jew-hatred takes many forms, but at its core is the belief that we should not exist.'

'No one is calling for the extermination of Israel,' Josh protested. 'We just want a state where everyone is equal!'

'Oh really?' replied Sarah. 'The annihilationist rhetoric used by your friends in the protest movement says otherwise. I just told you about the objectives of the BDS movement. And don't forget the anti-Israel protesters who broke into the Baillieu Library at the University of Melbourne. They spray-painted "Long Live the Intifada, Glory to the Resistance", and other anti-Semitic slogans on the walls. But let's say I give them the benefit of the doubt. Have a look at how religious and ethnic minorities are treated in Arab countries. Have a look at how Coptic Christians in Egypt, or Yazidis and Chaldeans in Iraq are all subject to pervasive persecution. A right of return would mean that Israel would become the majority Arab state of Palestine where Jews lived as a minority. How do you think they would fare?'

'You switch arguments so quickly you make my head spin,' Josh said. 'Who mentioned right of return?'

'Your friends do,' replied Sarah. 'Constantly. Look, kiddo, at the end of the day, anti-Zionist activists are either naïve or malicious. Either they ignore the brutal realities faced by ethnic minorities throughout the Middle East, or they actively desire to see the elimination of Israel's Jewish population. There's no third option.'

'That doesn't follow! What have other ethnic minorities got to do with criticism of Zionism? You're saying it's impossible to criticise Israel without demanding it should cease to exist. That's patent nonsense.' Josh sighed and concentrated on his smoked salmon.

'Nevertheless, I'm afraid to say your fellow protesters and the BDS satisfy all Sharansky's markers for anti-Semitism. Behind all the rhetoric of human rights, there's the desire to eradicate Israel as the nation-state of the Jewish people.'

Josh arched an eyebrow. 'Rubbish.'

'Don't you think the best way to foster Jewish–Arab coexistence is through shared day-to-day interaction?' challenged Sarah. 'But that's what the BDS movement seeks to stop. It pressures businesses to avoid Israelis and for companies to leave the West Bank. The West Bank has 2.9 million Palestinians and about 464,000 Jews. So, who do you think suffers more from BDS?'

'Now we're back to BDS?' said Josh.

'Maybe the example of Rami Levy will help,' said Sarah. 'He's an Israeli supermarket owner who's been harassed by the BDS movement for opening supermarkets in the West Bank that employed local Palestinians. Never mind that those Arab workers were paid double local salaries. Levy was trying to promote understanding by creating financial opportunities for Palestinians. But he cancelled that expansion plan because of political pressure. And now, BDS activists are targeting the peace agreements between Israel, the UAE and Bahrain.'

'They're pretty active at uni,' Josh said.

'As are Queers for Palestine,' Sarah snorted. 'More like Queers for Suicide.'

Josh tried to control himself but couldn't and broke into a snort of laughter. 'I have to admit that the Queers for Palestine thing has always struck me as ridiculous.'

'Yes, they're absurd,' said Sarah. 'But this is a serious issue. What about that friend of yours … what's his name … the flamboyant one with the English boyfriend?'

'You mean Sam?'

Sarah nodded. 'Yep, he's the one. How long do you think he'd survive in Gaza? Don't you know that there's an entire community of gay Palestinians in Tel Aviv who had to flee their homes to escape death by stoning at the hands of their families?'

'You're using the gay rights issue to justify Zionist oppression of the Palestinians,' Josh said.

'That's just another stupid woke slogan,' said Sarah. 'The fact remains that Arab society in general, and Palestinian society in particular, is violently homophobic. Hamas views homosexuality as a crime worthy of death by stoning. Petty theft is punishable by the amputation of the hand, and anybody who speaks badly of Islam can be put to death. They're Islamic fundamentalists with a worldview straight out of the Middle Ages. They view women as lesser beings who should be killed for besmirching the dignity of their families. Ever heard of honour killing?'

'Of course I've heard of it,' said Josh, 'but Hamas and the Palestinians aren't the same thing.'

'Conservative Arab society has a very rigid code of sexual behaviour for women,' said Sarah, pressing on. 'Violations are seen as a stain on family honour that can only be expunged through murder, which is committed usually by the father or brothers. Hundreds of Arab girls and women are killed each year because they had unapproved boyfriends or refused the marriage matches selected by their parents. That is Hamas. That is what you're defending.'

'Hundreds?' said Josh, pulling out his phone and typing rapidly. 'It looks like the bulk of so-called honour killings are committed in Pakistan … your figures aren't supported at all,' Josh protested.

Sarah was tapping away on her own phone. 'Know what George Orwell said? Let me find the quote … yeah, here it is: "Pacifism is objectively pro-Fascist. This is elementary common sense. If you hamper the war effort of one side, you automatically help that of the other." He wrote that in 1942, and what was true during the Second World War is equally true today. Besides, what about your own community?'

'Wha-a-a-t? Honour killings, pacifists, and now the trans community?' Can we stick to one topic? Explain to me where Israel's war effort has been hampered,' Josh demanded.

'The Biden administration, European Union and others are exerting pressure on Israel. They're pressing for an immediate ceasefire, which would ensure the continued existence of Hamas. And they were warning against Israel continuing its offensive into Rafah,' Sarah said.

'What about it?' Josh said.

'This constant Israel bashing by the UN gives anti-Israel activists a false sense of legitimacy that reaches all the way onto uni campuses and beyond. Don't forget, Jews are only two per cent of the American population, but they suffer over 50 per cent of ethnic and religious hate crimes. Since October 7, anti-Semitism is surging. People are once again drawing up lists of Jews. Jewish businesses are being attacked and boycotted by bad online reviews, negative social media posts and direct intimidation. There are demands to boycott Jewish-led companies and organisations. This is the sort of stuff that would make Goebbels proud. It validates my belief that Jew-hatred is like a dormant virus in Western society. It can lie low for a long time, but in the right circumstances it bursts forth with poisonous power.'

'So, now we're back to anti-Semitism. Mum, I think you must win by exhausting your opponents through the number of times you change the subject!' Josh shook his head. 'I'm starting to worry about your mental health. And what did your boss have to say after last night's performance?'

Sarah shrugged. 'Look, Josh, at the end of the day, I'm a Zionist. I am also sympathetic to the plight of the Palestinian people, so there is nothing I want more than to resolve the conflict.'

Josh snorted in disbelief and pushed his empty plate away.

'First, Hamas has to be destroyed and a responsible government installed that has the best interests of the Palestinian people at heart. Measures to attract private capital should be implemented so the Palestinians aren't so reliant on international aid and support.'

'Any ideas on how that can be done?' asked Josh.

'The Masri family in Ramallah has become a powerful part of the Palestinian economy. They funded and built Rawabi, an entirely new city in the West Bank. The city was built on the hills just outside Ramallah, north of Jerusalem. Hopefully, this is a first step towards a self-sufficient future – a future of industry and economic empowerment.'

'That would be nice,' said Josh dryly.

'People like Israeli peace activist Rabbi Froman believe that the way to reduce conflict in the region is to initiate meetings between settlers, Left-wing activists and Palestinians. He established a grassroots movement called Land of Peace to achieve this.'

'Did it work?'

'Too soon to tell. He passed away a decade ago, but his wife, Hadassah, is carrying on. By the way, did you know it's written in the Quran that the Jews will return to the Promised Land. "And thereafter We – God – said to the children of Israel: Dwell securely in the Promised Land."'

'Really? That surprises me,' Josh said.

'It surprises a lot of people,' Sarah said with a smile. 'They'd also be surprised to learn that Jerusalem isn't mentioned once.'

'In the Quran?' asked Josh.

'Yep,' Sarah nodded. 'Look, Israel is a force for good, Josh. You must see that. Israeli innovations have made the world a better place. Let me mention a few,' she went on, tapping away at her phone.

'No need, Mum,' Josh said with a sigh. 'Really!'

'Let's see … the first firewall was developed in Israel. ReWalk Robotics is helping amputees walk again and Waze technology is used by 100 million people for directions. In agriculture, Israel is responsible for drip irrigation technology, and in medicine and health Alpha Omega is the world leader in neuroscience and functional neurosurgery and Medicol created the heart stent. Israel is a world leader in water desalinisation and—'

Josh held up his hands. 'Okay, Mum. I get it. Israel does a lot of good in the world.'

'Remember when I mentioned the aid Israel provides to the Third World?' asked Michael.

Josh nodded.

'Well in 1957 Israel established the MASHAV, its Agency for International Development Cooperation. In addition to sending advisory teams worldwide, MASHAV brings people from sub-Saharan Africa to Israel for training. They provide courses in early childhood education development in Ghana, beekeeping courses in Rwanda, drip irrigation in Kenya, they're establishing neonatal units in Ghana, trauma units in Haiti and an eye hospital in Nepal, to name just a few.'

'I see what you're saying, Dad,' nodded Josh. 'But the same could be said about America. It does a great deal of good, but tell that to the Iranians or the Chileans, Nicaraguans ... You still don't seem to want to accept that legit criticism of Israel can be anything other than anti-Semitism.'

Sarah shrugged. 'As I said earlier, I think the Sharansky model is a good one. By that standard, the modern Left is without doubt anti-Semitic.'

Josh gave a long sigh. 'Nothing like a sweeping generalisation,' he said.

'Israel has become the main target of the modern Left. Zionism is hated by so-called anti-colonialists, anti-imperialists and anti-racists even though the creation of the Jewish state is neither colonial, imperialist nor racist. In fact, I would argue that Israel is the ultimate anti-colonialist success story.'

'That's absurd,' Josh said.

'Is it?' challenged Sarah. 'Remember when I described how Israel was created out of the ruins of two empires, the British and the Ottoman? The Zionists had to fight against the Brits in order to establish the Jewish state. But by falsely framing Israel as a settler colonial interloper in the Arab Middle East, the new anti-Semites can pose as the good guys. As the academic David Hirsh wrote, "Today's anti-Semitism is difficult to recognise because it does not come dressed in a Nazi uniform and it does not openly proclaim its hatred or fear of the Jews." But that doesn't make their Jew-hatred any less toxic.'

'Guys, we've been at this for almost an hour,' sighed Josh. 'And it's the same old song and dance. Is this really why you brought me home for dinner? A dinner that must be drying out in the oven, by the way.'

Sarah and Michael exchanged a long silent glance before she spoke. 'There's something else,' she said in a low tone. 'Something we've been keeping from you.'

'What?' frowned Josh. 'Are you guys getting divorced?'

Michael laughed. 'Nothing like that, son. Your mum and I are very happy.'

'But what we're about to tell you might make you less so,' frowned Sarah.

'So enough with the suspense,' said Josh. 'C'mon guys, out with it.'

Another glance between husband and wife was followed by the sound of Michael clearing his throat.

'Okay, son. During the mid-1990s, just after completing med school, I volunteered for a year with Médecins sans Frontièrs in Lebanon.'

'Doctors without Borders,' said Josh. 'They're a great organisation!'

'They do good work,' nodded Michael. 'But I was there in Lebanon with an ulterior motive.'

'What do you mean?' frowned Josh.

'I've never told anyone this, and it would be dangerous for me if the facts ever got out. But I have to tell you that as I was treating patients, I was also ... gathering intelligence.'

'For Israel?' asked Josh in a tone of disbelief.

Michael nodded. 'On Hezbollah and other militia groups that were waging war against the IDF.'

'So you were a Zionist spy?!'

'That's one way to describe it, I suppose,' shrugged Michael. 'But I prefer the term Jewish patriot. The information that I was collecting saved lives.'

'The lives of Israeli soldiers occupying Lebanon,' spat Josh. 'Imperialist aggressors in the service of Zionist expansion.'

Michael shook his head. 'The only reasons Israel invaded Lebanon in 1982 were to stop cross-border attacks by the PLO and establish an autonomous enclave to serve as a security zone.'

'Another one of those defensive wars that always happen to end with Israel gaining more territory?' Josh sneered.

'The Israelis withdrew from Lebanon in 2000 and the region was taken over by Hezbollah,' replied Sarah.

Josh got to his feet. 'And you were part of all this?' he said to his father. 'I … I'm going to need to process this,' he added.

Sarah got up and placed her hand on his arm.

'You're our son, and we love you. We may disagree on this issue; we may see the world very differently, but at the very least we agree on one thing: we'll always be a family. Can we please call a ceasefire?'

Josh gave his mother a peck on the cheek and walked out of the house without a word.

7

Somewhere neutral

'I still can't believe it,' Josh muttered into his pillow as he lay across their bed.

'I can,' shrugged Miryam. 'After all, they're rusted on Zio-fuckin' Nazis.'

'Whoa there,' Josh protested. 'They don't share our values, but they're still my mum and dad.'

'I've heard you say things almost as bad,' said Miryam.

'Yeah, but they're *my* mum and dad.'

'Well, sometimes we have to be willing to sacrifice personal ties for the sake of our beliefs,' Miryam said.

Josh snorted. 'I don't see you cutting off your family, despite the fact they aren't exactly exemplars of progressive principles.'

'What the fuck do you mean by that?'

'C'mon,' scoffed Josh. 'Your mum goes to mass at least three times a week. Your brother stood for the Liberals at the last state election. Not to mention the fact that Lebanese Maronites were allies of Israel during the civil war of the 1980s.'

'That's when my parents left,' said Miryam. 'To get away from all that.'

'Yeah sure. And that's why your brother was endorsed by Tony Abbott. Not to mention the fact that you keep our relationship in the closet. My parents would be fine with us if it wasn't for the political stuff. Yet you've avoided telling yours about me, and what that means, because you know they'd absolutely freak. So before you badmouth my parents again, look a bit closer to home, eh?'

'You're an asshole,' Miryam muttered.

'Maybe,' shrugged Josh, 'and you're a fucking hypocrite, which makes me something else as well.'

Miryam's brow furrowed in a quizzical frown.

'It also means I'm a fool. My love for you has blinded me to the path we've been following. I still have my family and my community in spite of everything …'

'Well, lucky you,' Miryam said snidely.

Josh sat upright on the bed in silence for a full minute before rising to his feet, then strode over to the dresser and extracted three days' worth of clothes, which he stuffed into a backpack by the bed.

'What are you doing?' asked Miryam, a note of panic creeping into her voice.

'I … I need to do some thinking.'

'But you can think here,' insisted Miryam.

Josh shook his head. 'Nah, I can't do it here or at home. I need somewhere … neutral. Maybe I'll go to my uncle Joe in Sydney. But I need to get away.'

'Please, Josh,' she begged, placing a hand on his forearm.

He shook it off and tightened the straps of his backpack.

'Will you call me, at least?' she said, her voice wobbling.

'I … I don't know,' Josh shrugged. 'Goodbye, Miryam.'

Then he opened the door and stepped out into the crisp Melbourne autumn night.

Acknowledgements

I n writing this story I was fortunate to have the support of many people. I am grateful for the help of my editors. Nan McNab and Ted Lapkin's extensive work in editing this story has been instrumental in making it infinitely better. I have greatly benefited from their insights, counsel and assistance. They have been remarkably patient with me, nothing was too difficult, and they were a pleasure to work with. I owe a huge debt of gratitude to them for their incredibly generous support. They gave willingly of their time and I have benefited from their understanding, acumen and direction.

Finally, many friends have been there for me along this journey. They are too numerous to name – you know who you are. Thank you for your support and encouragement. And last but not least, thank you to my family who have helped me keep everything in perspective.

About the author

Bernard Marin AM was born in 1950 and graduated from the Prahran College of Advanced Education in Melbourne in 1970. He established his accounting practice in 1981 and currently works with the staff and partners of the practice as a consultant.

Bernard has held a number of positions on various boards, including: Treasurer – Melbourne Writers Festival (2005–16), Koorie Heritage Trust (2000–12) and Liberty Victoria (1984–92); Board member – Australian Centre for Jewish Civilisation (2009–15), Reichstein Foundation (2011–12) and Melbourne Community Foundation (2009–10). He lives in Melbourne with his wife, Wendy.

By the same author

My Father, My Father
Good as Gold
Stories of Profit and Loss
Stories of Remembering and Forgetting
Letter to My Father
People Who Have Changed the World:
Imagined Interviews
We Had a Dream
Breakfast with Paul: We Beg to Differ
Surviving: My Story
Burning Leaves

**These titles can be found at
www.bernardmarin.com.au**

www.ingramcontent.com/pod-product-compliance
Lightning Source LLC
Chambersburg PA
CBHW032013180726
48283CB00008B/2655